BROKEN-HEARTED ON BLACKPOOL SANDS

Copyright © 2024 Rebecca Paulinyi

All rights reserved

This is a work of fiction. Names, characters, businesses, places, events and incidents are either the products of the author's imagination or used in a fictitious manner. Any resemblance to actual persons, living or dead, or actual events is purely coincidental.

No part of this book may be reproduced, or stored in a retrieval system, or transmitted in any form or by any means, electronic, mechanical, photocopying, recording, or otherwise, without express written permission of the publisher.

Cover design by: GetCovers

For my husband, who did propose to me on a beach! (Torcross, not Blackpool Sands)

CONTENTS

Title Page
Copyright
Dedication
Chapter One — 1
Chapter Two — 6
Chapter Three — 14
Chapter Four — 18
Chapter Five — 24
Chapter Six — 29
Chapter Seven — 34
Chapter Eight — 46
Chapter Nine — 54
Chapter Ten — 59
Chapter Eleven — 67
Chapter Twelve — 76
Chapter Thirteen — 84
Chapter Fourteen — 92
Chapter Fifteen — 96
Chapter Sixteen — 105

Chapter Seventeen	112
Chapter Eighteen	117
Chapter Nineteen	126
Chapter Twenty	135
Chapter Twenty-One	139
Chapter Twenty-Two	146
Chapter Twenty-Three	155
Chapter Twenty-Four	160
Chapter Twenty-Five	170
Chapter Twenty-Six	175
Chapter Twenty-Seven	179
Afterword	187
Dreaming of Devon	189
Books By This Author	193

CHAPTER ONE

Ivy Thompson never expected to still be living in her childhood bedroom at the age of twenty-five – but that was just the way her life had gone.

She wasn't miserable about the fact; she loved living in the South West of Devon. She got on with her dad better than anyone she knew got on with their parents, and her boyfriend only lived in the next village.

But running the family dairy business with her dad didn't pay all that well, and housing in Devon was pricey. Especially as she had no desire to live with housemates.

And so somehow the years had passed by and she had stayed living – and working – with her dad, and feeling pretty content about it.

So she didn't tend to stop at the estate agent's window when she was walking to work. But on that damp spring morning, as she walked up Kingsbridge high street in order to open the little shop that she and her father had rented earlier that year in order to sell their cheeses and milk, she did stop.

And one flat caught her eye.

The rent was crazy – but that wasn't what she noticed first. It was the view from the living room window.

She could see the sea.

Sure, it was in the distance, and pretty tiny, and the

place only had one bedroom. But Ivy had loved the beach, and the ocean, for as long as she could remember, and the thought of being able to see it from her home made her heart soar.

Maybe...

Maybe it was time to think about the future.

She stared at the listing for a little longer, and then hurried up the hill to open up the shop.

Her dad – along with a couple of locals – ran Colebrook Farm, out of which Colebrook Dairy had grown. At first, they had sold milk, cheeses, and creams from the farm itself. Then, last summer, they had started up the delivery service – and things had just gone from strength to strength since then.

Ivy still did a lot of the deliveries herself, but with the number of local businesses they now supplied, it wasn't possible for her to do it all.

Especially not since they had acquired the shop. It was only small, and they did not open every day of the week, but it was generally always busy.

Ivy split her time between delivery driving, the shop, and seeing her boyfriend on her days off.

Life was very busy – and, come to think of it, her wages had rather increased too.

She couldn't afford the rent on the flat in Dartmouth by herself... But she could certainly manage half of it.

After all, there was no reason that she and Jackson shouldn't live together. It was bizarre, really, that they didn't already. They had been dating since they were seventeen – well, there'd been a couple of brief break-ups in the middle, but neither of them counted those.

But every time the topic of moving in together had

come up, there had been reasons for it not to happen.

Dad had needed more help on the farm. Jackson had just lost his job as a manager in the local supermarket. The housing market was bad.

There were always reasons – and Ivy had never really questioned it.

Until now. Now, she could not stop thinking about where her life was headed, and the next steps she would take.

For a long time, she had harboured the romantic notion that one day, Jackson would propose to her on her favourite beach, Blackpool Sands. They had spent so many days there together in the summers, and evenings too, having barbecues after work.

It just seemed like the ideal place for a romantic proposal.

She had loved the beach for far longer than that. It was the beach she remembered her mum taking her to as a little kid. A beach full of happy memories – and she wanted to add another to them.

But in the years since this dream had first sprung up in her mind, marriage had not really been discussed. She had never moved past the daydream.

But maybe moving in together was a step in that direction. Maybe it would show Jackson that things ought to be moving forward.

"How much for those, dear?"

Ivy blinked rapidly and realised with embarrassment that she had not noticed the old lady coming in, choosing some cheese, and standing at the till.

"I'm so sorry," she said, rushing to ring up the purchases. They had an old-fashioned till that her dad had bought at an auction one day, and it always proved popular with the customers. Privately, Ivy would have preferred a computerised one that worked out the price and the change for her – but she knew this antique was far more popular. Besides, she hated to do anything that upset or disappointed her dad.

Ever since Mum had died when Ivy was only eight years old, they had been a team of two. They didn't argue, they didn't disagree, they didn't talk about much in depth. And their lives continued on, smooth enough, but always with the gaping hole that Mum had left.

"You're a proper dolly daydreamer today, aren't you," the customer said, but Ivy was relieved to see a smile on her face. People around here were generally pretty friendly – but she wasn't one to be so unprofessional, normally.

"I am so sorry. One of those days. That's six eighty, please – and here, try this sample of our new yoghurt. We're really excited about it."

Ivy was relieved that the shop was fairly quiet that morning. It gave her time to get lost in her thoughts without having to apologise. Once the season started, and the kids broke up from school, there would be no let-up. The whole of the South Hams was extremely popular with tourists, and the dairy shop would undoubtedly be heaving.

That evening, she texted Jackson, excited at the thought of sharing her plan with him. He wasn't one for talking much, and certainly not about his dreams, but she was hopeful that this would get him thinking about the future.

If not, she thought she would have to drop some heavy hints. Because, really, how many years did he expect them to be dating before they moved things forward? Ten?

"Penny for your thoughts, love?" her dad, Steve, said as she cleared up from dinner that evening. There had been no response from Jackson, but that wasn't unusual. He was always pretty useless at staying in touch.

"Just thinking about life," she said with a laugh.

Dad smiled, his blue eyes crinkling. "Nothing major, then," he said with a laugh of his own.

The business was doing so well, and she loved taking a leading role in that. She loved Jackson, too – although she wished she could see more of him.

She was happy – but did that mean she couldn't want more in life? She didn't think so. She didn't want to leave Devon. She'd never wanted to. Even when all her friends had left for uni or jobs or relationships. She'd always wanted to stay here, and she still did. She just didn't want to stay *exactly* where she was forever.

CHAPTER TWO

"Are you up to anything nice this weekend, love?" Dad asked over breakfast that morning.

"Well, if you weren't insisting I take a day off, then I would be working," Ivy said with a laugh. She opened her boiled egg with a satisfying crack.

"I know the business is going great, and I know that's mainly down to you – but you have to take some time off occasionally. You'll burn yourself out otherwise. And anyway, isn't Jackson wondering where you are? Haven't seen him in a little while."

Ivy sighed. Although she was the one working crazy hours, Jackson had been less communicative than usual of late. She hoped there was nothing really bothering him. He had a tendency to get in his own head about things and not talk about them until they became a bigger issue than they needed to be.

"He's working," Ivy said with a tight smile. She didn't actually know if that was true – but it was easier than explaining to Dad that Jackson was just being a bit useless.

"That's a shame."

Ivy nodded and salted her egg. Dad always made the perfect hard-boiled eggs. When they were both home at breakfast time – which was not often, really, with Ivy busy with deliveries and the shop, and Dad taking care of the farm – they would sit and eat breakfast together.

"I've been invited to a housewarming, though," Ivy said with a shrug. "I wasn't sure if I was going to go…"

"You definitely should," Dad said enthusiastically. "Whose housewarming is it?"

"Do you remember Christi, who runs the campsite in Salcombe with her aunt?"

"Olivia Noakes, isn't it? I remember when she moved down here…"

Ivy smiled. She was never totally sure if it was a good or a bad thing that everybody knew everyone and that nothing was ever a secret in this place.

"Yeah, that's the one. But she's dating Oscar Reynolds – the gardener? Landscaper? I'm never quite sure what he does."

Dad nodded, taking a bite into his slightly burnt toast. That was the way he liked it, apparently. He thought Ivy's toast was anaemic – but he always did it the way she asked for.

"Yeah, he's a nice guy. A handy man to be dating, too." He laughed at his own joke. "Handy. Handyman. Get it?" Ivy rolled her eyes but laughed along with him.

"Well, they've bought a big old house in Malborough together. I can't quite remember where. I think they plan to turn it into a hotel or something – needs a lot of work."

"Sounds like an exciting project," Dad said.

"Yeah, it does. Christi and I have got on since I started delivering there, and they're having a housewarming, even though the place isn't ready to live in yet."

"Well, that's your weekend plan sorted then," Dad said with a grin, and Ivy supposed going wasn't a terrible idea. She didn't know many of the people who were invited, but she enjoyed spending time with people. There was no use obsessing over why Jackson was being so rubbish at the minute.

He'd figure it out, and everything would go back to normal. It always did.

Ivy drove up the long, winding drive that led to the house Christi and Oscar had purchased. She had to check its location on a map before she left because, although she had driven through Malborough many times, she didn't know the village all that well.

The dairy's deliveries were mainly to businesses, and so the housing areas were not well known to her.

The house was an impressive three-storey building, with more windows than Ivy could accurately count with a quick glance. She couldn't quite remember what Christi had said their intentions were with the place when they had discussed it. Christi had turned around Sunset Shore Campsite, making improvements and using her knowledge of marketing to make the place a must-visit site for campers coming to the South West. And with Oscar's DIY skills – well, Ivy had no doubt they'd make this place a success, no matter what exactly they planned to do with it.

The drive was already filled with cars, and she had to block in a couple in order to park. For a moment, she wished Jackson had come with her. Not because she was shy, because she generally felt very comfortable around large groups of people. If anything, she tended to talk too much.

No, she wished he was here because she was going

to have to explain why he wasn't. She'd been dating him forever, and anyone who knew her knew him too. What was he so busy doing that he didn't have time for his long-time girlfriend? If she wanted to share the answer, she couldn't, because she just didn't know.

She raised a hand to knock on the heavy oak door, but it swung open before she had a chance to. The hallway was decorated in a very seventies style, but structurally it looked pretty sound – well, to Ivy's very uneducated eye, anyway. At the other end, the living room was filled with people – and Christi King rushed out to greet her.

"Ivy!" she said with a warm smile. "You came!" Ivy grinned.

"Had to see what this place was like, didn't I? It's massive, Christi. I didn't realise quite how big you meant."

Christi blushed. "I know. And it's so much work – down here is okay, if you can ignore the decor, but upstairs needs so much work. Oscar and I are going to turn the office down here into a bedroom, so that we can live here while we get the rest of the place up and running."

At the mention of his name, Oscar Reynolds appeared from a room Ivy presumed was the kitchen, a beer in his hand. "Hey, Ivy. Can I get you a drink?"

"A coke or something would be great, I'm driving," she said by way of explanation. "Sorry that Jackson couldn't make it," she said, belatedly remembering the invitation had been to both of them.

"I'm glad to see you here. You always seem to be so busy working."

Ivy laughed. "You want to talk. Every time I deliver to the campsite there's some new improvement that you've masterminded. Is the summer looking busy?"

Christi grinned. "Heaving. We might have to take on more staff. I can't really believe it's all worked out..."

"Well, I can. Olivia must be thrilled."

"I think so. Although she likes to go on about it being too much work for a woman at her age – as if she ever looks any older. She's here somewhere, probably eyeing up where would be a good location for one of her murals. I think we got her a bit obsessed with doing them, after we started it at the campsite."

Oscar returned with a can of coke for Ivy and then wrapped his arm around Christi's waist. Ivy tried to ignore the lump in her throat at the sight of how happy they were. They were lovely people. They deserved to be happy. Oscar Reynolds had been a few years above her in school, and he'd always been the guy everyone fancied. Ivy had probably had a crush on him herself at some point, although not in any serious way.

But he'd never settled down – until Christi had come to town, just for the summer, and something had grown between them. Now they were building up businesses together, buying houses, starting their lives. They'd only been together what, a year? And here she was, coming up to eight years with Jackson and no sign of a house, a ring, the proposal she'd always dreamed about on Blackpool Sands beach...

She forced the thoughts from her head and smiled at the happy couple. "Remind me what the eventual plan is here?"

"Well, it's going to take a lot of work, but we're aiming for it to be a B&B, in the end," Oscar said, with a grin in Christi's direction. "We figured that we managed to do pretty well with the campsite, with Christi's ideas and my muscles—"

Christi giggled and batted his arm.

"So we've pooled our resources and taken on this massive project."

"We'll be needing cheese and milk delivered once we're up and running – so make sure you've got room for us in your busy order books," Christi said with a smile.

Ivy let the hosts get back to mingling and wandered the room with her can of coke, happily chatting to other guests and looking at the very *interesting* decor. She couldn't tell if it hadn't been updated since the seventies, or if the previous owners just had very retro tastes – but she was intrigued to see what it would look like when Oscar and Christi had finished with their work on it.

It was amazing how Christi had planned to be here for the summer, and ended up choosing to settle here permanently, Ivy thought, as she checked her phone and found she had no new messages. She and Jackson had messaged a handful of times over the week, but she really wasn't sure what he was so busy with.

The supermarket closed at nine, but perhaps he was taking extra shelf-stacking shifts? Maybe he needed to save up for something?

She told her stupid, romantic, optimistic heart to calm down as Olivia Noakes, Christi's aunt, headed in her direction.

Just because he was working more, didn't mean he was thinking about their future.

Just because she was thinking about what their next step should be, didn't mean he was on the same page.

She would just have to make sure he knew where she wanted them to head.

She didn't want to still be living at home in a year's time, seeing her boyfriend on her nights off like she was still a teenager. She wanted a committed relationship, living together at the very least.

Maybe more.

She wanted to stay in South West Devon, definitely – but she also wanted a plan. Not to get stuck living life in exactly the same way they had been doing for the last eight years.

"Ivy, how lovely to see you," Olivia said with a warm smile that lit up her eyes.

"And you, Olivia," Ivy said, leaning into the hug Olivia offered. "What a beautiful dress!" It was covered in daffodils and it lit up the room as much as Olivia's smile did.

"Thank you. I'm amazed to see you having some time off!"

Ivy laughed. "You're not the first person to say that," she admitted. "But there's not much dairy work to be done at this time on a Friday night, anyway. So I don't feel too guilty about being away from it all…"

Olivia tutted. "You should never feel guilty for taking a break, dear! Work to live, don't live to work!"

"I do love building up the business, though," Ivy said. "But Dad says I need to take a break every now and then, so I suppose you're right!"

"I definitely am," Olivia said. "Although, my niece doesn't listen to me. I manage to get her to take some time off and what does she do? Goes and buys a house that will take up every spare minute of her free time." Olivia glanced in Christi's direction, and although her words were admonishing, there was a smile on her lips.

"They look very happy though, don't they," Ivy said. She couldn't help but voice it. There was a glow about the two of them that seemed to announce how content they were with the way their lives were going.

When she'd talked to Christi on the beach last summer, and Christi had said she was moving away, that glow had definitely not been there.

Christi had given Devon, and love, a chance, and thrown herself into a new life with everything she had.

Ivy didn't want a whole new life. Just a new direction. And she was determined to steer her and Jackson to a new course.

CHAPTER THREE

When she had not seen him in a full ten days, she decided it was time to take the bull by the horns. There was busy, and then there was just distant. She'd been working a lot, and so had he – but every text exchange was started by her, and every response he sent was short.

She'd had enough of it.

She'd known, pretty much since she'd started dating him, that Jackson Shaw didn't like being confronted. He liked to do things in his own time, and to come to his own decisions, and he did not like to be questioned or persuaded in any way.

But they were a team. A partnership. And if she wanted more, she was going to have to ask for it.

Summer was fast approaching, and as she pulled out her phone on her lunch break in the shop, sun glinted through the windows and reflected off the screen.

Haven't seen you in a while! Everything okay? Xxx

She slunk into the back room as she waited for a reply, noticing people milling around outside the door. The shop wasn't big enough to need two employees, but that did mean she had to close up for ten minutes so she could get a break. At the beginning, she had continued serving without noticing the time. And then, even when she did notice, she didn't like to close up, in case it meant they lost a sale.

But by the end of the second week, she had nearly fainted – and Dad had made her promise that she would take a break every day to at least grab a sandwich.

If she stayed in the shop, though, people tried to come in, and she ended up serving them. So it was better to go for a walk, or sit in the tiny back room where they kept their stock. She never took her break over the lunch period, when shopkeepers would come and buy the cheese sandwiches that they sold, or pick up some milk for the rest of the day – but there always seemed to be someone who wanted to come and shop, no matter what time she took her lunch.

She picked at her sandwich – which was cheese, of course, made in their own dairy – and stared at her phone, willing him to respond. She was just going to turn up at his place if he didn't reply today, she decided. She wasn't some casual fling he could just ignore when life got too much.

She was his girlfriend. She'd been with him for *years*. She loved him.

Then it buzzed, and her heart leapt.

Sorry, it read. *Been busy. When's your next day off?*

Ivy grinned. She'd been worrying for nothing. He was just busy – and, now that she had reminded him, he wanted to make plans.

I can do Wednesday if you can? Xxx she replied, knowing that he often had Wednesdays off.

Unusually, the reply was almost instant.

Can do. Weather is supposed to be nice. Where shall we meet?

Her favourite place in the whole of the South Hams – probably the whole world, if she was honest, although she hadn't explored very much of it – popped into her head.

Blackpool Sands? I could bring a picnic. Xxx

She was already planning it in her mind when he replied. She glanced up at the clock on the wall and hurried to finish her sandwich. The customers would be waiting for her – she had only put a 'back in ten minutes' sign on the door, and she was in danger of going over that.

Of course, it was unlikely anyone had seen exactly when she'd put it up – but still, she didn't want to keep anyone waiting.

Sure. Meet you there at twelve? We can have the picnic and talk.

Those words stuck in her head as she served customers for the rest of the afternoon.

Was this it? Was he finally going to want to move things forward?

Was there any chance he would propose?

She had definitely mentioned to him, over the years, how romantic a beach proposal – and more specifically, a proposal on Blackpool Sands – would be. Was he finally ready to commit to their future?

She felt giddy at the thought. She'd doodled 'Mrs Ivy Shaw' on her pencil case in secondary school, on her planner in sixth form, and even once she was too old to doodle it, she'd thought about it.

They were meant to be. Everyone had always said it. They'd started dating at seventeen, and been serious pretty much from day one. With no siblings, and her mum gone, Ivy had often felt lonely, no matter how hard Dad tried to be there for her. He had the farm to run, and that was time-consuming work.

Jackson had been there. And then he had stayed in Devon too, when everyone had gone off to live their adult lives. They had stuck together, outlasting any of their friends' teenage romances.

She wanted to marry him. To start a family of her own. She dreamed of a big family, of a house filled with children and chaos and laughter. She loved her dad so much, and appreciated the mammoth task he had accomplished of being both parents to her – but their home was quiet, and calm, and she wanted something different for her future.

Could Jackson finally be ready to pop the question she had been awaiting for so long?

CHAPTER FOUR

Ivy was very pleased when Wednesday morning dawned dry and sunny. You never could predict what English weather would be like – and, being so close to the sea, Devon was even more unpredictable.

She was up early enough to see Dad heading out to milk the cows. It had been a long time since she helped with that side of the business, with the deliveries and the shop taking up so many hours.

Dad grinned. "Morning, sweetheart. I hope you're up this early because you're doing something nice with your day off, not to work."

"It's so lovely and sunny, I couldn't sleep in," Ivy said, beaming. "But I have actually got plans – I'm meeting Jackson for a picnic on the beach." As she poured boiling water into two mugs, she could barely contain her excitement. In the days since they had arranged to meet, she had convinced herself that he was going to propose.

She didn't want Dad to catch on to how excited she was, though, and ask questions, so she tried to keep still and go about the morning as usual.

"That sounds nice. Beautiful day for it too. I'm glad to hear Jackson is putting in a bit of effort."

Ivy rolled her eyes. "You know what he's like, Dad. He gets wrapped up in what he's doing, loses track of time. But he always comes through when I need him."

Dad nodded but changed the topic of conversation. "Will you be home for dinner?" he asked, taking the mug of tea off her with a word of thanks.

"I'm not sure," Ivy said, feeling a little giddy. If he did propose, there would be so much to talk about. So much to celebrate… "I'll message you, let you know. There's a shepherd's pie in the freezer, though, if I'm not back in time."

"You don't need to worry about me all the time. I can cook for myself, you know. If I have to…"

"Yeah, yeah, I know. But it's there if you want it." Ivy had been cooking dinner every night since her early teens. She didn't remember there ever being a discussion about it… Just that one day, after Mum had died, the meals delivered by well-wishers had dried up – and Ivy had realised that her Dad really didn't have a clue how to cook. He made great boiled eggs, but that was about his limit.

But Ivy did know how to cook. And she enjoyed it too. They'd got along together pretty well, really, over the years. She felt a twinge of guilt at the thought of leaving him to fend for himself. Well, only if Jackson proposed. She gave herself a mental shake. Even if he didn't propose, she was planning to move in with him, wasn't she? Presuming she could persuade him it was a good idea, anyway.

Dad would have to cope on his own – and for the first time, she wondered whether he had ever considered marrying again. Not just to have someone to look after him, but for some companionship. She hadn't expected to stay living at home for this long and certainly didn't want to be doing so forever.

But then maybe Dad could look after himself, and

he just chose not to, because there was no need.

"Well, these cows won't milk themselves," Dad said, jerking his head towards the front door. "Have a good day, love."

Ivy grinned, kissed her dad on the cheek, and set to work making the picnic. She wanted everything to be perfect.

She made sandwiches with their award-winning cheddar and some pickle she had bought from a lady who lived down the road and made her own. Then she made some ham ones too, because she knew Jackson liked them.

One of the reasons she had got up so early was so that she could do some baking, and she happily made scones, humming to herself as the sunlight shone through the farmhouse windows.

Today was going to be a very good day.

She considered putting on a bottle of champagne – or at least prosecco – but thought that might look like she was expecting too much, and so settled on two cans of Coke and a mini bottle of wine to share. After all, they would both be driving. And if there was celebrating to do, that could be done afterwards. Elsewhere.

It didn't take long to drive from the farmhouse on the outskirts of Slapton to Blackpool Sands, and she was pleased, because twelve o'clock was suddenly approaching very quickly. She changed into a clean outfit – a flowery dress that she hoped didn't look too dressy but which would certainly be too much for a day working in the shop or delivering – and hurried out the door, nearly forgetting the picnic as she did.

At the back of her mind, a worry began to niggle. What if he didn't propose? What if she was imagining all of this because it was what she wanted?

Well, she told herself, she would just have to steer things in that direction. If he wasn't going to take the initiative, she would. Perhaps she would propose... although she wasn't sure her old-fashioned Jackson would like that very much. She would at least seriously broach the topic of moving in together.

There were a handful of cars in the little car park when she arrived, thanks to the beautiful weather. In a few short weeks, the place would be heaving with tourists, but for now, it was only locals enjoying a walk, taking their dogs out, or letting their kids run around on the beautiful golden sand.

How lucky she was, she thought as she stepped out of the car and wandered towards the edge of the beach to wait for Jackson, to have all of this right on her doorstep. Who would ever want to leave?

It was ten past twelve by the time Jackson's beaten-up Landrover pulled up into the car park. Ivy jumped up from the wall she had been perching on, leaving the picnic basket there, and rushed over to him.

She didn't like going so long without seeing him.

She threw her arms around him as she approached and he gave her a one-armed hug back. "Sorry I'm late."

"It doesn't matter," Ivy said. "Isn't it a beautiful day?"

"Feels like summer is here," Jackson agreed, glancing up at the blue sky. He ran a hand through his dark brown hair, and looked down at her. The height difference between them meant she spent her life on tiptoes, looking up into his chocolatey eyes.

"I've missed you," she said, reaching to press a kiss to his lips, before taking his hand and leading him towards the picnic basket.

He didn't speak as they found a spot and she spread out the red and white checked blanket she'd found in a cupboard at home. Ivy closed her eyes for a moment and soaked up the sunshine. Her heart felt at peace here.

When she was younger, she'd not realised that for some people, a day at the seaside was a rare event. When Mum was still alive, and sometimes if Dad had some free time, they would come down to the beach after school on a nice day, and dip in the water to wash off the sweat of the day.

Once Ivy could drive, it was the first place she had driven herself to completely alone.

She couldn't imagine living away from the beautiful expanse of water that she had lived near for her whole life. Not being able to take off her shoes and scrunch her toes in the sand whenever she liked... The beach always reminded her of Mum, of happy memories, of her heart soaring and the sun shining.

Realising her mind had been wandering for far too long, she took a seat next to Jackson on the rug and leant against his solid arm. "So. How's your week been? You've been pretty quiet."

"Yeah, sorry. Things just got a bit crazy..." He trailed off, and she waited to see if he wanted to add any more, but he simply fell silent.

"I know what you mean," she said, wishing she didn't always have to keep the conversation going. "The shop is busier than ever, and the deliveries seem to be getting further out, too. The other day I had to drive to Goveton – you know, out towards Totnes? Yeah, and there was a massive lorry stuck in the lane. I had to reverse all the way back and do a massive detour." She rolled her eyes. "Those lanes are not built for lorries that big, but I guess their sat-navs send them that way..."

She knew she was babbling, but she hated awkward silences. And Jackson was a pretty quiet man – so she often ended up filling the space with inconsequential chatter.

She felt nervous, and she was sure it was showing. She had convinced herself he was going to propose, and she wanted him to feel comfortable enough to do so.

Ivy just wanted everything to be perfect.

CHAPTER FIVE

"Let's eat," Ivy said, wanting something to do. She unpacked the vintage picnic basket that had been her mother's, and her mother's mother's, long before it was hers. "I made ham sandwiches for you," she said, laying them out. "And there's some Coke in there, if you're thirsty?" She didn't mention the mini bottle of wine. She'd pull that out later. After.

Jackson ate the sandwiches and said they were good and they both watched as a surfer got pulled under by a wave, before popping back up again.

"I saw an amazing flat in the window of the estate agents," she said, feeling the need to push the conversation in some sort of direction.

"Oh?"

"Yeah. Got me thinking. I don't want to live with Dad forever. I mean, I love him, and the farm, but at some point I don't want to have to ask if my boyfriend can stay over!" She laughed. *Hopefully not boyfriend for much longer,* she thought to herself.

Jackson bit his bottom lip and Ivy thought it was cute how nervous he seemed.

"Don't you think?"

He nodded. "Yeah. Yeah, that makes sense."

She didn't expect him to suggest they move in together. He never did anything spontaneously. But at least the seed had been planted…

"I'm just… I feel like everything is going the way it's meant to, don't you?" Ivy said, opening a can of Coke and taking a sip. "The business is going well, and I feel like it's time to focus on what I want for the future." She reached over and took his hand. "What we want for the future."

Jackson cleared his throat and blinked. "You're right," he said. "We should think about that."

Butterflies filled Ivy's stomach, and she squeezed his hand tightly. This was it. She was on the most beautiful beach in the world, with the man of her dreams, and things were all going exactly as she'd planned.

He slid his hand out of hers and moved to put a little space between them. Ivy took a deep breath and waited expectantly.

"I should have said this sooner," Jackson said, fiddling with the blanket and avoiding making eye contact.

"That doesn't matter now," Ivy said. *Better late than never!*

"Ivy… We've been together a long time. Grown up together, practically."

Ivy grinned. Yes, they had a long history together – and she couldn't wait for their future to begin.

"And over that time… Things change. People change."

Ivy stopped a frown taking over her features just in time. She didn't want to ruin the moment – but she wasn't sure where he was going with this.

"I need a change," he said, and it was the most forcefully he'd ever said anything before.

"Okay," Ivy said, feeling a little unsure. "I get that. I don't want everything to stay the same, either." *I want to marry you. I want to live with you. I want to have children with you.*

"I don't know how to say this. But… I'm moving away."

Ivy swallowed, her eyes frozen wide, her heart racing.

"What?"

"I'm moving. Leaving Devon."

"What do you mean, you're moving?" Ivy asked, her brain whirring back into action. "You can't just tell me you're leaving. We're a couple, we make decisions together."

Jackson took a deep breath. "I need to be clear. I'm leaving…and we're done."

Ivy felt as though her heart had shattered into a thousand pieces inside her chest. On the outside she looked whole, but inside, she was destroyed.

"What?" This time her voice was hoarse and quiet, and there were tears welling in her eyes.

"I'm sorry, Ivy. I am. But…"

"Please don't do this," Ivy said, hating herself for begging, but unable to let him go. She reached out to take a hold of his hand again, clinging on to him. "Jackson. We can talk about this. You want a change, we can change things. I can come with you, if you really have to leave. We don't have to—" Even though she knew it would break her heart to move away, it was the only thing she could think to offer.

"No." His voice was sharp, and he wrenched his hand from hers. "Ivy. Don't make this harder. You're not listening. I'm leaving. Without you. I…" He paused. "There's someone else. I met her online. She lives in Birmingham."

"You-you-" She couldn't get the words out. Nothing made sense any more. Here she was on the most perfect beach in the world, and Jackson was saying these terrible things that made no sense.

How could he say there was someone else? They'd been together forever. They were going to get married. They were Jackson and Ivy.

Birmingham? The place stuck in her mind. The training course that Jackson had been on the previous month. That had been in Birmingham.

And the stag do for his best mate, back in March.

"No," she said, shaking her head. "No, this can't be, you can't, I don't—"

Jackson stood up. "I am sorry, Ivy. I really am. I wish I had told you earlier."

Tears began to fall uncontrollably from Ivy's eyes, and she had to remind herself to breathe. *No. No. You can't just be sorry you didn't tell me earlier. You can't just walk away. After all these years…*

"I'm in love with her, Ivy. I've handed in my notice. I leave next week."

And then he walked away, ripping her heart from her chest as he did so.

Ivy sat and watched him until he was out of sight, and then let the sobs rip through her. At least the beach was pretty empty. No one would come and see if she was okay.

Because she wasn't okay.

She would never be okay again.

Did he know that the only way she would accept that it was really over was by telling her such a painful reality – that he was in love with another woman?

Or did he just want to hurt her?

She didn't know how long she sat on her favourite beach, crying and staring and wishing that she could rewind this day and change the outcome somehow.

But there was nothing she could do to repair her broken heart.

CHAPTER SIX

Ivy didn't know how she drove home. She almost felt drunk – even though the small bottle of wine remained unopened in the picnic basket.

After all, there wasn't anything to celebrate.

She replayed the conversation over and over in her mind on the short drive back home. She tried to look at it from every angle, to consider any alternative meanings – but there were none that she could find.

Jackson was in love with someone else, and he was leaving Devon.

Leaving her.

When she pulled up outside the farmhouse, she managed to check the time on the car clock. She had totally lost track of the time since she had arrived at the beach. The time before. The time when she was full of hope and happiness.

It was five-thirty. She had been sitting and moping on the beach for hours. Dad would certainly be home, and probably heating up the cottage pie that she had told him was in the freezer. As he got up so early to milk the cows, he always ate dinner early, before going to bed early too.

She didn't know how to face him. She and Dad didn't talk about their emotions. They had a great relationship, but not one that allowed for discussions about matters of the heart.

But she had to go in. It was her home. Where else was she going to go? After all, she wouldn't be moving out now. This was her life, maybe forever. The spinster at home with her father.

If she hadn't been feeling so broken-hearted, she would have told herself to get a grip. That she wasn't living in some Victorian novel. That being single did not mean her life was over.

But right now, that was exactly how it felt.

She glanced at herself in the rear-view mirror. It would take a hell of a lot of make-up – and far more than she had on her – to hide the fact that she had been crying. She wasn't even sure a full night's sleep would get rid of the bloodshot eyes.

There was nothing she could do. She would have to get past Dad somehow, and then take herself to bed. Maybe things would look better in the morning.

She carried the vintage picnic basket with her as she climbed out of the car. She threw the contents back in it on the beach, no longer caring whether everything looked perfect. But even heartbroken, she did not want to end up with rotten cheese in her car.

She took a deep breath before pushing the door open. Dad only locked it when he went to bed, and he even forgot then, sometimes. It wasn't unusual for people in Devon, and considering how isolated they were, Dad never seemed very worried about burglaries.

Now, when it came to his prize cattle, he felt a bit differently. They were always locked away at night – just in case.

"Ivy?" Dad called from the kitchen. "Is that you?"

As if it would be anyone else. It had just been the two of them for so long – and now it looked like it would be the two of them forever.

Ivy choked back a sob.

"Yeah, it's me, Dad," Ivy said, trying to make her voice as normal as possible.

"You're back early. I thought you were going to message! How was Jackson?"

Even the sound of his name was painful, and Ivy winced as she made her way down the corridor to the kitchen. She had to put the basket down, and she couldn't just disappear off to her room without saying hello. Then Dad would know something was up, and he'd probably feel the need to come up and talk to her about it. That would be far more awkward than a conversation in the kitchen.

"Ivy?" Dad said the moment she walked into the room. There was concern in his voice, and she realised he was more perceptive than she gave him credit for.

"What's the matter? What happened?"

Ivy swallowed. She did not think she could tell him the whole story. She wasn't even sure she could give him the headline.

"I'm fine," she said, even though it was a lie, and it wasn't even what he had asked.

"Are you sure? You don't look it. Did Jackson…" He trailed off, and Ivy wondered what he imagined Jackson had done. Was Ivy the only one completely blindsided by her boyfriend of eight years ending things?

She had been so convinced that he was going to propose. Surely there had been signs that had led her in that direction. Surely she hadn't invented the entire idea herself?

"We…" She put the basket down on the kitchen counter and sighed. "We're done," she said, the words even more painful to say than she had imagined. "I don't want to talk about it, but Jackson and I are finished." She couldn't hold back a sob, and Dad half rose from the table.

"I'm going to bed, Dad," she said, even though it wasn't even six o'clock yet. "I'll be okay. I just need some space."

Ivy didn't really believe that that was true. How could she be okay? She had spent so many of her best years with a man who had fallen in love with another woman. A man who, it seemed, had been in love with another woman for quite some time, and just hadn't got around to telling her.

A man she had thought she would marry, and who now she was unlikely to ever see again.

But she couldn't talk about any of that with Dad. And so she said goodnight to him, grabbed the miniature bottle of wine, and disappeared to her bedroom.

This can't be real, she thought to herself, as she downed the bottle in two gulps and wished she had a full-sized one.

She'd spent eight years of her life with Jackson. He was the only person she had ever slept with. She'd only kissed one other guy. She knew her life seemed sheltered, but she'd been with the same man since she was seventeen. There hadn't been any reason to play the field because she had been happy. She had been with the man that she planned to spend the rest of her life with.

And now, apparently, he'd changed. She'd changed. *They'd* changed. And he didn't want her any more.

How could he be in love with someone else?

How could he tell her so coolly that he was leaving?

Tears poured down her cheeks. She pulled out her phone, hoping desperately that Jackson might have rung, that he might have changed his mind – but there was nothing. No messages, no calls.

He meant it.

She didn't even bother to get undressed, but instead cried herself to sleep, hoping that things would look brighter in the morning.

CHAPTER SEVEN

The only thing that had changed in the morning was that her eyes were red and sore and difficult to open. She couldn't remember falling asleep, and when she woke up, she didn't initially remember why she was in her clothes, or why her face was so puffy.

Then it all came flooding back, and her heart ached once more.

She glanced at her phone, like she did every morning, and choked back tears at the fact that there were still no messages. And it was already nearly seven. Dad would be out milking, and she had deliveries to get on with. At least it was a day that the shop was closed. It would be far easier to hide her misery from people if she was just dropping off crates of cheese and milk, than standing behind the shop counter on display.

Dragging herself into the bathroom, she turned the shower up to hotter than she would normally like it, and let the steaming hot water wash away the sand and tears from the day before.

Jackson's face wouldn't leave her mind. His cold, determined expression when he said he was leaving. That he was in love with another woman.

Was he going to marry this woman? Have children with her? Was she going to live the life Ivy had always planned for herself?

As she got out, dried herself, and began to pull the hairbrush through her long, knotted brown hair, her thoughts turned to what she could have done to prevent this disaster.

Maybe if I had pushed for us to move in together sooner, she thought as she pulled her hair up into a bun. *Or not pushed when he went quiet for days on end. Or maybe if I'd been more adventurous, wanted to move away…*

She was very glad when she got to the kitchen that Dad was still out in the cowshed. She wondered if he was avoiding her – he never knew how to deal with her when she was emotional, and she didn't want to discuss it.

Usually, Ivy packed up the crates for delivery the night before, and stacked them in the industrial-sized fridge in the dairy. Since she hadn't been in the right frame of mind the previous night, she expected the crates to be in the hallway empty, but they were nowhere to be found.

When she got to the van, she almost smiled at the fact that it was already packed and ready to be driven. Dad must have done it before milking the cows, in the early hours of the morning.

He wasn't very good at speaking to her about how she felt, but she knew that he cared. His actions always spoke much louder than words.

He was coming in from the barn when she started the engine, and she raised a hand to wave goodbye, hoping her red, puffy eyes weren't obvious from this distance.

The radio drowned out her thoughts and she blasted it as she wound through the narrow lanes. The van had no air con, and even though it was early, the day was already warming up nicely. She cracked the windows open and thought about how much she had been looking forward to the summer.

But what was there to look forward to now? Most of her early deliveries were businesses that simply signed to say they'd received the box and barely looked up – and she was very pleased with that state of affairs. If someone had asked her if she was okay, she was pretty sure she would have just burst into tears. And that wasn't very professional.

When she got out to Salcombe, the sun was reaching its highest point in the sky, and Ivy's stomach reminded her loudly that she had not eaten since the ill-fated picnic the day before.

Sunset Shore Campsite had been pretty quiet before the owner's niece, Christi King, had come to stay for the summer and had implemented loads of new ideas. She hadn't planned to stay – but things had taken off for her, both with the business and with Oscar, and so she had stuck around. Now, of course, she had the house in Malborough too, and so Ivy never knew if she was going to be at the campsite when she brought the twice weekly deliveries for their campers and the little shop they had on site.

Today, she hoped Christi wouldn't be there. They got on well – Ivy even thought they could be called friends, even though they'd not known each other for years and years. But Christi would surely notice something was wrong, and ask, and then Ivy wouldn't be able to hold herself together until she got safely home.

She knocked on the cottage door, where Olivia Noakes lived, and felt her heart drop when Christi answered the door.

"Brilliant," she said with a grin. "We've just run out

of milk. You're an angel. Here, let me take that."

It was only when she came back to the door to sign the invoice that Christi's eyes narrowed.

"Ivy? Are you okay?"

"I—" She couldn't even answer. There was no way she could say yes. And if she said no...

Well, she'd have to elaborate.

"You're clearly not okay," Christi said, before Ivy had to answer. "Come in, have a cup of tea. We've got milk now!"

"I really should be getting back," she said, glancing back at her van, which was blocking in a fancy-looking sports car. She wondered if Christi had suddenly decided to learn to drive. But if she had, Ivy couldn't imagine she would have chosen a car like that. Money aside, the shiny red exterior would be scratched up after a week of driving around the Devon lanes.

"You can spare twenty minutes," Christi said. "You really look like you could do with a cuppa. And a chat."

And with that, she managed to propel Ivy through the door, and Ivy found herself sitting at the big oak dining table, her heartbreak ready to spill from her mouth the second she was probed.

Christi busied herself making the tea with the old-fashioned kettle that Olivia still used – one that went on top of the Aga and whistled when it was done. There was an old-world charm to it, although Ivy thought she would probably forget about it and wander off, leaving it to boil dry. She was so scatterbrained sometimes. She was definitely better off sticking with her trusty electric kettle.

"So," Christi said as she poured boiling water into a teapot. "Do you want to make small talk for twenty minutes? Or do you want to tell me what's wrong straight away?"

Ivy let out a strangled laugh. Christi had definitely not been so direct with her when they had first met. But since then, Christi seemed to have grown used to Ivy's hundred-mile-a-minute conversation style – and she had become more blunt with her opinions.

"I—" Ivy struggled to find the words as Christi sat opposite her and pushed a cup across the table.

She met her friend's green eyes and the words came tumbling out.

"Jackson broke up with me," she whispered, almost as if, by not saying it loudly, it wouldn't be real.

But it was real.

Tears pricked at her eyes at just saying the words. Christi reached out across the table and grabbed her hand.

"What? Seriously?"

Ivy nodded glumly.

"Just like that? What did he say? Ivy, I'm so sorry, I…"

Ivy didn't know if it was helpful or not to rake over it all again, but Christi's indignation at him ending things out of the blue certainly made her feel a bit more understood.

Dad would have been on her side, of course, if she'd told him what had happened.

But he wouldn't have known what to say. He might have even threatened to go around and beat him up, even though that was very un-Dad, because he thought it was the right thing to say.

But it wouldn't have been.

"Just like that," Ivy said. "And I even thought…" She choked back a sob. She couldn't tell her. It was too ridiculous.

"What?" Christi asked, squeezing her hand.

Ivy shook her head. "Never mind." It was too embarrassing. *I thought he was going to propose. I thought he was the man I was going to spend the rest of my life with.* "He's leaving Devon. Moving to Birmingham, apparently. Because..." The next part was also embarrassing, but she knew she had to tell Christi. She needed someone else to know the heart-breaking, terrible reason Jackson had decided it was over.

"He's in love with another woman," she whispered. "He's moving to live with her."

Christi's eyes widened. "What? That— How dare he! After what, ten years?"

"Eight," Ivy said miserably. "What's wrong with me?" she asked in a small voice. "What has she got, that I haven't? Oh god, don't answer that, I know how pathetic I sound. I just..."

"You do not sound pathetic," Christi said, pouring them both a cup of now well-stewed tea. "He's the coward in all of this. Telling you that he's in love with someone else and then just leaving. People change, people fall out of love – he should have told you he wanted to call it quits months ago, if there was someone else in the picture."

Ivy let go of Christi's hand and sat up a little straighter. Christi's strong words helped her to feel a little more sure of herself. What Ivy wanted was for Jackson to be in love with her, to marry her, to want to stay with her forever. But if he didn't want that, she supposed he was entitled to feel that way.

But to string her along for God knew how long, and then tell her there was someone else?

That was the worst bit of all.

"He doesn't deserve you," Christi said, pushing a glass bottle of Colebrook Dairy's milk towards her. "But I know that probably doesn't make anything better right now. When was this?"

"Yesterday," Ivy said, watching the milk mixing with the strong tea. "On Blackpool Sands."

"On your favourite beach?" Christi said with a gasp. "Your favourite place in the world? What a—"

The front door flew open, cutting off whatever expletive Christi had planned to say, and Ivy jumped. Her head snapped round to look at who had entered, quickly wiping her eyes with her sleeves as she did so. She was relieved to see it was only Christi's aunt, Olivia, dressed in a bright blue dress covered in sunshines that made Ivy smile without even meaning to.

"Sorry, lost control of the door!" Olivia said with a grin, kicking it closed behind her. Her arms were filled with an assortment of footballs and frisbees. "Found all these out on the field. Thought we could clean them up, get rid of any that aren't salvageable, so the kids this summer can play with them."

"Good plan," Christi said, jumping up to help her aunt. "That swing set was popular over Easter, too – reckon it'll be busy when the summer holidays start!"

"Definitely. Sorry, Ivy, I didn't mean to just ignore you. Lovely to see you."

"And you, Olivia," Ivy said, hoping her eyes weren't red from the tears she knew had been building there, threatening to fall.

"I think your brother's back from his walk into town," Olivia said to Christi. "I don't want to interrupt you two though, I just thought you might want to see if they've eaten…"

Christi laughed and rolled her eyes. "He's a big boy, I'm sure he can get his own lunch. But yes, I'll go and see how they're doing." She glanced over at Ivy and narrowed her eyes. "Why don't you come with me, Ivy?"

"Oh, I should be going," Ivy said, hurrying to finish her lukewarm tea. "I didn't even know your brother was visiting. That's nice!" She was not in the mood to socialise, which was quite unusual for her really, and the last thing she wanted was some pity-filled attempt at matchmaking.

"It is – and the first one of the three who's made it down here! Of course he's dragged his mates with him, couldn't cope with boring rural Devon on his own, but he's here." She grinned, and Ivy knew that she wholly disagreed with her brother's view of the area. Three brothers…that sounded exhausting. And nice, too. No loneliness with all those siblings, Ivy was sure.

"They're staying in that fancy yurt we put in at the top of the hill," Christi said. "I'll take them some tea, could you just help me carry it up? Say hi, you'll be off in ten minutes, promise."

And how could she say no?

◆ ◆ ◆

Christi loaded up a tray with three mugs of tea, and handed a plate of biscuits to Ivy to carry. Ivy rather thought that Christi could have managed it all on her own – but it seemed a bit rude to suggest that.

She followed Christi up the steep field, which had tents dotted all over it. Even though it was only May, and not in the school holidays, the campsite was still pretty popular. Not sold out, but certainly not empty.

That was all down to Christi, Ivy was sure. Before

she had come, the campsite had been pretty run down, and whenever Ivy had gone out that way, she had noticed how empty the field was. Not now, though. Christi had thrown her heart and soul into the place. The shower block had been renovated, and a beautiful ocean mural covered the building. There was a firepit, a bar, a hot tub, swings, a little shop... The place was thriving.

And, of course, the latest addition: the luxury yurt that had been installed at the top of the hill. Christi had told her that they'd invested a fair amount of money into it, after having done everything else on a shoestring budget. Ivy was sure they would make the money back though in bookings: the wooden yurt was beautiful. And it was perfect for people who wanted to be out in nature, but didn't really like camping.

People, apparently, like Christi's brother.

Christi handed her the tray of teas when they reached the yurt – proving Ivy's point that one person could have managed them – and hammered on the door. Ivy glanced out over the ocean, which was glittering in the spring sunlight, and sighed. This was a happy place. She usually felt happy when she came here. But today, her heart ached and she just wanted to run away.

"Don't break the door down, sis," a male voice grumbled as the door opened. Ivy tore her eyes away from the sea to be greeted by a dark-haired man pulling a t-shirt over his rather impressive muscles.

Christi sighed and rolled her eyes. "Stop exaggerating. Aren't lawyers meant to tell the truth, Anthony?"

Anthony laughed. "They're meant to defend their clients. Not the same thing at all."

"I brought up tea and some of Aunt Olivia's

biscuits," Christi said, reaching out for the tray and the plate from Ivy. Ivy forced a smile, feeling awkward. Normally she always had something to say, but today that was not the case.

"Thanks. We've been swimming, I'm starving." The door swung open to reveal two more men – thankfully fully dressed – behind him, seeming to agree wholeheartedly. They were polar opposites of one another: one had olive skin and short dark hair, where the other was fair with a mop of blond hair, and piercing blue eyes.

"Aunt Olivia's always got a full fridge, if you're starving," Christi said. "These biscuits won't keep you going for long." She handed them the plate and, sure enough, each man grabbed two and it was soon empty.

Ivy laughed in spite of herself.

"Oh, Ivy, sorry. This is my brother, Anthony, and his friends..." She paused for a moment and bit her lip. "Alfie and Simon?"

"We would have been very offended if you had forgotten our names already," the blond-haired man said with a cheeky grin.

"I'm a busy woman," Christi said. "With important things on my mind."

"Yes, yes, we know you're a thriving businesswoman," Anthony said with a good-natured smile. "It's nice to meet you, Ivy. Do you live around here then?"

Ivy nodded, feeling surprisingly flustered at all eyes being on her. It was because she was so miserable, she was sure. Normally, she always had something to say.

Although the three men were unusually good-looking. Maybe she would have been tongue-tied around them anyway.

"Over in Slapton," she said.

"He's a city boy," Christi said with another roll of her eyes. "He barely made it here. And he's too scared of scratching his precious sports car to travel very far."

Ahh, Ivy thought to herself. *It's his sports car. That makes more sense.*

"It's beautiful here," the dark-haired man said. "Really picturesque. And the weather..."

"Well, it's not always like this," Ivy said with a laugh. "But I wouldn't want to live anywhere else."

"Ivy brought some more milk and cheese from her dairy, after you so kindly polished the milk off this morning, *Tony,*" Christi said. Ivy wasn't used to being around siblings, but neither of them seemed bothered by the good-natured ribbing.

"Oh, that cheese yesterday was incredible," the blond man said. Ivy wished she knew which was Simon and which was Alfie, just so she could get them straight in her head.

"Thanks," Ivy said, grinning as she always did when Colebrook Dairy was praised.

"Did you make it?"

"I might have done. Or my dad. It's a family business..."

"It'd be worth risking your car for some more of that cheese," the blond said, digging Anthony in the ribs.

"If Anthony can't manage driving on the lanes, I'm sure Oscar will take you to the Colebrook Dairy shop," Christi said.

"Oh yes, loverboy to the rescue," Anthony said, and Christi gave him a shove.

"We deliver here," Ivy said in a small voice. "If you're

still around on Sunday. I can bring more with me..."

"Perfect, thank you. I have to take some back to Oxford when we go."

"You only think with your stomach, Alfie," Anthony said.

"I do," Alfie said, not looking embarrassed by this at all. He gave Ivy a warm smile that sent a shiver through her that she didn't quite understand. "I like good food. Is that a crime?"

"I suppose not. Let's get some lunch then – otherwise I won't hear the end of it."

As she drove home that afternoon, Ivy was grateful to Christi for dragging her in and hearing her out and telling her that she had done nothing wrong. It was what she needed to hear, even if it couldn't fix her broken heart. The distraction of the bickering between the siblings, and Christi's brother's handsome friends, had also stopped her thinking about Jackson, at least for a little while.

But now he was on her mind again, and as she pulled up at home, she wanted so badly to text him, to ring him, to know how his day had been and to make plans to see him.

But she couldn't.

And so, by the time she entered the kitchen, her heart was heavy again. And this time, Dad wasn't going to let her just run away and cry in her room alone.

CHAPTER EIGHT

On the kitchen table were two packages wrapped up in paper, and from the smell of vinegar in the air, Ivy knew instantly what was in them.

"Alright, love?" Dad asked, smiling cautiously. "I picked up fish and chips from the van down in the village. They might need heating up, but I thought you might not fancy cooking…"

"Thanks, Dad," Ivy said. The chair squeaked as she pulled it out from under the table and sat down, reaching for one of the packets. It felt warm enough and so she opened it up and put a vinegary chip into her mouth with a sigh.

"How's your day been?" Dad asked, opening up his own fish and chips and immediately adding more salt to them.

"The usual," Ivy said, wondering if she should bring up Jackson, get the conversation over and done with, or whether if she ignored the topic for long enough, it would just go away.

"And you're in the shop tomorrow, aren't you?" Dad asked when Ivy didn't fill the silence with chat. Ivy pulled off a piece of fish with her fingers, not bothering to get up and get cutlery. She had noticed today how often there were silences that needed filling. Normally, she would rush to do so – but she just couldn't right now. It was too much to think about.

"Yeah." She glanced up at her dad and saw him wince at her brief answer, and so she tried to make more of an effort. "How was your day?"

"Busy, as usual," he said with a grin. "The gate in the barn got stuck, took me a while to get it fixed."

Ivy nodded and chewed her chip as if the task needed all of her concentration.

"Look, I don't want to pry, sweetheart. But if you want to talk..."

Ivy shook her head, feeling tears springing to her eyes at even the thought of Jackson, let alone having to discuss their awful break-up.

"I'll be okay," she said in a strained voice.

"Of course you will," Dad said, far more confidently. "You were too good for him anyway."

Ivy cracked a half smile. "You have to say that. You're my dad."

"I'd say it anyway. And if you want me to go and speak to him—"

Ivy shook her head violently. "No. Don't do that. He's entitled to not want to be with me any more. It hurts, but it is what it is."

Neither of them mentioned Jackson's name over the next few weeks. Ivy threw herself into work with even more vigour than she normally did. She got to the shop well before opening and made sure the place was spotless. She advertised their delivery service everywhere she could, and then took on the extra deliveries herself. She didn't take a day off, and she only slept for a handful of hours each night. Anything to help her forget how miserable she was.

It was probably the first time in her life that

she found herself wishing that she lived somewhere else. Somewhere anonymous. Because word got around pretty quickly that she and he-who-must-not-be-named had broken up – and people weren't shy about asking questions.

Or giving unnecessary opinions.

The weekly visit to the dairy shop in Kingsbridge from Mrs Sloane, a resident of the town that Ivy had known since she was born, was a particular low point. The first week she asked if the rumours were true, and Ivy had been forced to say that yes, they were.

The next week she had been treated to a twenty-five-minute lecture on how Mrs Sloane had known all along that they wouldn't last, and that they weren't right for each other, and that she ought to have known that a relationship from her teenage years wasn't going to last forever.

Ivy tried to smile and nod and not let out the stream of angry words that filled her head.

Doing her deliveries wasn't much better. She didn't go down to Blackpool Sands beach, even though the weather was particularly beautiful, because it would hurt too much – but every time she drove along the coastal path, her eyes strayed to the golden sands, and her heart broke all over again.

With the advertising she had been doing, her deliveries took her further afield, and she started a regular delivery to the quirky town of Totnes. The first time she visited the newest customer, a little café called 'Carol's Café', the owner insisted she sit down and have an iced coffee, and she felt rude refusing – even though she tried very hard not to have any time to sit and think.

"I've been using your cheese in our savoury scones,"

the owner said as she brought over the drink to a little table in the window. "And everyone has commented on it. We might need to up our deliveries!"

Ivy grinned. "That's always good to hear!"

The bell dinged above the door as it flew open, and two children, pursued by a man in a police uniform, raced in. The café owner glanced around and laughed.

"Mummy, Mummy, Daddy wouldn't let me sit in the front," the boy cried, clinging to the woman's apron. Ivy thought he was probably about five, although she had never been great at guessing kids' ages.

"I didn't want to move the car seat," the man said, leaning in to kiss the woman on the cheek.

"Can I have a milkshake Mum?" the girl asked.

"Sorry," the owner said, turning to Ivy with a roll of her eyes. "Always chaos. I'll be in touch about those extra deliveries though, okay?"

"Definitely," Ivy said, watching as the woman ushered away the two children.

The ache in her heart intensified as the family laughed and joked together. It was what she had imagined for herself, in the future. A business. A husband. Kids.

And what did she have now?

The business, she supposed – although it was technically her dad's, not hers.

She'd always thought everything would work out the way it was supposed to. When her friends had left to go to uni or to travel or to start over in a big city, she had told them she was very happy staying where she had grown up.

And it had been true.

But she'd had a clear picture in her mind of where

it would all end up. Eight years of dating *him* and she'd presumed they were heading in that direction. That one day she would have the family she dreamed of.

And now...

She just felt empty. She didn't know if the things she had always wanted were still the things she wanted.

She'd obviously been wrong about Jackson.

Maybe she'd been wrong about everything.

◆ ◆ ◆

Although Ivy had kept in touch with quite a few of her old school friends who had long since left Devon, she couldn't bring herself to confide in any of them about breaking up with Jackson. She was sure several of them knew – after all, most of their parents still lived in the area, and it certainly seemed to be the hot topic of gossip around town.

But none of them rang her or messaged her about it, and she was relieved. She'd thought she'd had it all. Everything she ever wanted, right there in the place that she loved most.

It was far too humiliating to admit that she had been totally wrong.

She hadn't seen Jackson since that day on the beach. She was sure he'd left for Birmingham now, but she had no way of knowing for sure. She certainly wasn't going to message him or visit his parents. She had spotted his mum once in the supermarket, but she had hidden in the freezer aisle until she disappeared.

The only person she really felt she could talk to was Christi, who invited her in again for a cup of tea the next week, and the week after that. Her brother and his handsome friends, it seemed, had left – but that didn't mean Christi had loads more time on her hands. With the busy season fast approaching, she was rushing around more than ever – but she always made time for Ivy, which Ivy appreciated more than she could ever say.

"What if that was it?" she asked on one cloudy day at the end of June, sitting in Christi's aunt's kitchen with a mug of tea in her hands. Ivy was pretty sure Christi lived most of the time in the house in Malborough with Oscar – but with the campsite so busy, she was often there, and still seemed to treat the cottage like home.

"What do you mean, 'it'?" Christi asked, screwing up her eyebrows.

"My one chance at happiness," Ivy said with a sigh. "My soulmate. True love. You know what I mean."

"I don't think he's your soulmate if he just up and left for someone else like that," Christi said with a frown. "And you're young, Ivy – I know you were in a relationship for a long time, but a lot of people don't settle down until much older than you. I know this is rubbish, but..." She tapped her fingers on her cup of tea and bit her bottom lip.

"What is it?" Ivy asked, sensing there was something her friend did not want to say.

"Look, I'm not usually the blunt one between us. But I think you need to think about whether things really were as perfect between you two as you're remembering."

"I didn't say they were perfect," mumbled Ivy, feeling a little attacked. She was sure her cheeks were turning red.

"No, I know, but – I always thought things in my life were pretty perfect. That my job was great, that I loved living in London... Until I was actually happy. Now I look back and realise I was just pretending that everything was perfect, because it was what I wanted to believe. Do you see what I mean?"

Ivy considered her friend's words for a moment. She had never claimed that things were perfect between them, but she *had* wanted to marry him. She had thought she would be happy being with this man forever... Had she been looking at things through rose-tinted glasses?

An uncomfortable feeling grew in the pit of her stomach as she remembered all the times she had wondered where he was, or why he wasn't responding, or why he never made much of an effort. Was she an idiot? Had she just been going along with a broken relationship because she was too scared to find anything else?

Her bottom lip wobbled, and she bit it to stop herself from crying.

"Oh, Ivy, I didn't mean to upset you. I just meant—"

Ivy swallowed and shook her head. "It's okay. I know what you meant. And you're probably right – but I don't really want to talk about that right now."

Christi nodded and sipped her tea, and Ivy did the same. For a few moments, there was simply silence.

"How are things with you, anyway? Did you get to spend some time with your brother? And how's the house?" Even if Christi's achievements reminded her of her own failings in life, at least they were a distraction.

"Yeah, it was nice to see him. It's the first time any of them have been down, just for a holiday. Mum and Dad came when they thought I would leave with them, but they haven't come back since. I've always felt like the failure—"

Ivy snorted. "You? A failure? That's ridiculous." Christi flushed slightly pink and laughed.

"You haven't met the rest of my family," she said

with a chuckle. "Lawyers, doctors, sports stars – believe me, I'm the failure. But it's okay. I don't actually feel like that any more."

"Good. You shouldn't. You've done amazing things here. And things with Oscar…"

Christi beamed, and Ivy couldn't help the flash of jealousy that shot through her body.

"It's great. The house is a lot of work, but we love it. I never thought…" She glanced out of the window, and Ivy's eyes followed hers to where the handsome figure of Oscar Reynolds was carrying a large, heavy-looking barrel across the field.

"I never could have imagined this. I didn't even know this is what I wanted. So please don't lose hope, Ivy. This is a setback, I know – but things will get better."

CHAPTER NINE

There were a few cloudy days, but in general the weather only got nicer as the busiest season of the year in Devon began: the summer holidays. Everywhere that Ivy went there were queues of people and traffic, and kids excitedly eating ice creams and running around in shorts and t-shirts. It was usually her favourite time of the year – but she was struggling this year to push away the dark cloud that was always above her.

She didn't really talk about it. She was so busy, she didn't have time to stop at the campsite for a cup of tea, and Dad certainly didn't bring it up.

Eventually, the local gossips moved on to someone else, and her heartbreak didn't matter to them any more.

She wished it didn't matter to her any more.

The only time she thought about Jackson was when she slept – and that was only because her traitorous mind had dreams (or nightmares, even) about him. She would wake up in a cold sweat after seeing him with another woman while she slept. The woman's face changed every time, but the two of them were always laughing at her. Stupid little Ivy, who hadn't had a clue that her boyfriend had fallen out of love with her.

Sometimes, when she was up before the crack of dawn, she went out to milk the cows. It was one less job for Dad to do then. Besides, she quite enjoyed their comforting, non-judgmental company. It was quiet and warm in the cowshed, and the repetitive task felt almost meditative.

When she went inside, planning to take a shower before making breakfast for her and her dad, she was met by Dad pouring coffee with a concerned look on his face.

"Morning, Dad," Ivy said, washing her hands and waiting for whatever Dad wanted to get off his chest.

"Ivy, honey, this is getting ridiculous," Dad said, exasperated.

Ivy frowned, actually completely in the dark as to what he was complaining about.

"You haven't had a day off since…" He trailed off, but of course Ivy knew what he was referring to. *That* day. "You don't sleep, you barely eat, you're thinner than I've ever seen you and you've got bags under your eyes—"

"Geez, Dad, thanks for making me feel worse than I already do," Ivy snapped back. It was the closest she could remember them coming to an argument in years.

"Ivy, you know that's not what I want to do," Dad said, running a hand through his greying hair. "But you're going to make yourself ill. You need to look after yourself. You'll get through this—" He closed his eyes briefly. It was the closest he'd come to mentioning the miserable state she'd been in for the last couple of months. "—but you cannot run yourself into the ground like this."

"I thought it would help, milking the cows," Ivy said in a quiet voice, sitting down at the table with her mug of coffee, suddenly drained of all energy.

Dad sat down opposite her. "You know it does, love. Everything you do helps. But that doesn't mean you need to do everything. Please, just take a day off. At least one. Do whatever you want. Sleep all day, if you like. Just don't work."

She had no choice but to agree – but she had no idea what to do with herself. She hadn't taken a day off in nearly two months, just as Dad had noticed. Since things between her and Jackson had crumbled to nothing.

In the shower, she let the hot water run over her body for far longer than usual, washing her hair twice and taking the time to shave her legs. Well, she thought she took a lot longer – but when she got out, it had only been fifteen minutes. That wasn't going to fill the day.

Dad had grabbed a bowl of cereal and headed out onto the farm, so there was no point in cooking a big breakfast. Besides, she didn't have much of an appetite. She did consider going back to bed, and she crawled back under the covers with her long brown hair still wrapped up in a towel, but it was no use. She couldn't sleep.

Although she had the time to do so, she couldn't be bothered to blow dry her hair. It was so long that she always felt really hot and bothered if she ever had to use the hairdryer and besides, she wasn't even sure where it was. Instead, she sat in front of her mirror and split it into two, plaiting each side. As she did, she contemplated redecorating her room. It had been the same shade of purple since she was seventeen. Maybe it was time for something a bit more grown up – since it looked as though she would be living there for the foreseeable future. There were still Blu Tack marks on the walls from where she had pulled down boy band posters at the point when she had decided she was definitely too old for those.

But she found she didn't even have the energy to think about what she wanted her room to look like. What she wanted her life to look like. And so that plan fell by the wayside, too.

◆ ◆ ◆

The drive along Slapton line was one of her favourites, and thankfully it did not hold any memories of him. Since she had learned to drive at seventeen, she had enjoyed driving fast along the straight piece of road, with the ocean to one side and Slapton Ley to the other. She always blasted the radio, rolled down the windows, and felt grateful for the beautiful place that she lived in.

She had done this with her friends, and even with her dad – but not with Jackson. It wasn't his sort of thing. She was grateful for that now, because it meant she could still enjoy it without thinking of him. So many things in her life were tainted now with memories of before.

Even though she was not in a positive mood, she stuck to her old rituals: windows down, radio on, and a good rev of the engine.

It didn't make her feel much better, but it didn't make her feel worse, either – and that was a bonus.

Torcross Beach looked heaving as she doubled back on herself to do the drive again, but she couldn't bring herself to stop. Before, with a sunny day off at her disposal, she would have got an ice cream and wandered along the beach, or had a dip in the sea. But she just couldn't bring herself to now. She hated Jackson for many things – and ruining the beach for her was quite high up on that list.

After that, she drove rather aimlessly, filling up with petrol when she realised she was getting low, and grabbing a chocolate bar at the petrol station when she realised she had not eaten all day.

She didn't really make a conscious decision to drive over to Salcombe. She was already in Malborough by the time she realised where she was heading. But maybe Christi would be free for a cup of tea, she thought to herself. Or she could offer to help out. The place was bound to be heaving, with the kids having broken up from school.

CHAPTER TEN

The only car in the driveway of the campsite's cottage was a sports car – and not the red one that Christi's brother had been so worried about scratching a few weeks earlier. This one was black and coated in a fine layer of dust from the dry lanes around the campsite. She couldn't see Oscar's truck or Olivia's car, and she wondered if they were all out. That would be unusual, though, especially at this time of year. Someone was always around to run the place – and she had hoped they might have some task she could do to kill some time. After all, she'd told Dad she wouldn't work, but if she was just volunteering, surely it was different.

There was no answer when she knocked on the front door. She was fairly sure that, if she tried it, it would be open, but she had no wish to. She wasn't going to sit in Olivia's cottage alone, when she had no idea when – or if – Christi would be back.

She wandered back towards her car, wondering what she was going to do with her time now. In the distance, she could see the ocean, glittering under the summer sunshine. A dip in the sea would be lovely…but she had not been to a beach, any beach, since *that* day. And she didn't think it would help her misery to go down to one today.

It would bring back too many memories. And make

her think about all those questions that she was so desperately trying to ignore. Was Jackson happy? Had he told this woman he loved her? Were they living together? Were they planning the rest of their lives together?

"They had to go into Salcombe to collect something," a voice said, disrupting her miserable thoughts. "They'll be back soon though. I said I'd take any messages..."

She turned and blocked the sun from her eyes to see who was speaking – and was surprised to find the tall, blond-haired friend of Christi's brother standing at the edge of the field. His blond hair fell just across his eyes and his smile sent warmth rushing through her.

"Hey, you're the one who made the amazing cheese, right?"

Ivy couldn't help but smile at the fact that he remembered her. "Yeah, that's me. And you're... Alfie, right?"

He beamed. "Yeah. Well remembered. It's Ivy, isn't it?"

"Yeah. I thought you guys were long gone!" Ivy said, trying to remember back to when she had met the three men. It had been May, she was sure – and although she had not been tracking time so well lately, she was pretty confident they had not stayed in that yurt for the last two months.

He laughed. "Oh yeah. It's just me this time – came back for some business, and loved this place so much I thought I'd stay again!" He winked at Ivy. "Plus I get mate's rates, since Anthony's aunt owns the place."

"It is beautiful," Ivy said, glancing over at the sea wistfully. "I'll head off, if they're not around. Thought I'd just see if they needed any help, since it's the busy season." The field was filled with tents and caravans, and she could see people in the far corner of the field using the hot tub. It really had become a must-stay destination.

"I was just about to have a beer," Alfie said. "I know, it's only lunchtime, but I am technically on holiday, and the sun is out..."

Ivy laughed. "The sun *is* out," she said. "And you never know how long that's going to last! Although we've been pretty lucky so far this year."

"We have. Come and join me – then you can see Christi when she gets back."

Ivy paused. The answer that jumped to her lips was no, because she didn't want to socialise with anyone lately.

But then she *was* looking for a way to spend the day.

"I'm driving," she said, still not sure whether she was going to stay.

"You can have one," Alfie said with a shrug. "I get that taxis probably aren't much of an option round here..."

"I'm not really a beer drinker," she said, trying to find reasons to decline. But his smile was so warm and the way he looked at her sent a tingle through her that she had not felt in a long time.

She felt guilty for feeling anything positive about spending time with a man, and then quickly pushed that feeling away. She wasn't sure she knew how to flirt – it had been so long since it had been necessary – but there was nothing wrong with her flirting with this very good-looking man, if she wanted to.

She was a free, single woman.

And she thought he was probably the most beautiful man she had ever seen.

"I've got some Coke," Alfie said. "Or I can get you something from the bar, I know where they keep the keys and they told me to help myself…"

"Coke is fine," Ivy said, her heart jumping as she decided that a drink with him might be a pleasant way to spend her time off. It wouldn't be for long, anyway. Christi would be back soon, and then Ivy could ask her what she could do to help around the campsite.

She followed Alfie up the hill to the wooden yurt where he had stayed before. He opened the door and stood aside to let her in first. Sunlight filtered through the windows, making the place feel rather magical.

"Have you been in here before?" he asked, going over to the mini fridge and pulling out a green glass bottle of beer along with a glass bottle of Coke.

"I had a quick look when it was first built," she said. "But not really since then."

"Have you seen out the back door?" he asked, handing her the drink, and gesturing to the door on the opposite side of the circular structure.

Ivy shook her head, then took the bottle from him with a word of thanks and put it to her lips. There was always something better about drinking Coke from a glass bottle.

"You have to come and see," he said with boyish enthusiasm, grabbing her hand and dragging her along with him.

She laughed and nearly spilled her drink. He flung open the door, and she was rather surprised to be met with a tiny garden, hidden from the rest of the campsite by trees, that was filled with wildflowers. The explosion of colour in the sunlight was breathtaking, and for a moment she forgot she was holding his hand, until he pulled her out into the little square patch of heaven.

Her heart began to race and her mind went blank as he dragged her out into the sunshine.

"It's just perfect, don't you think?"

She nodded, her mouth going dry. "Perfect."

"And if you look through those trees," – he took their joined hands and pointed in the direction he meant – "you can even see the sea, on a nice day like this."

The wildflowers formed a horseshoe around a small patch of grass, on which two wood chairs were placed, and Alfie dropped her hand as they took a seat.

Ivy was rather taken aback by his enthusiasm for life. Most people were more reserved... well, except for her, she supposed. Usually, she was the one waxing lyrical about how beautiful something was.

But she'd been struggling to see the beauty lately.

No one could deny the beauty here, though. She wondered why Christi had never shown her this amazing little private garden for the yurt before. She imagined it took a lot of work to keep it looking this beautiful, even though it was tiny. It was, she thought, probably Oscar's work. Maybe Christi didn't even know how wonderful it was.

"Have you known Christi long?" Alfie asked, sipping on his beer and watching her intently with his icy blue eyes.

"Since she moved down here, I guess," Ivy said, trying to think back to the first time they'd met, when she'd come to deliver a sample crate of dairy goods. A lot had changed since then.

"Sounds like she shocked her family, deciding to leave London and come down here," Alfie commented.

"I hadn't met any of them until you lot came down

the other month," Ivy said with a shrug. "But she loves it down here. I'm glad she stayed."

"I can understand the appeal," he said, not taking his eyes off her. "I'm a city boy, and I won't deny it, but there's something about this place…"

Ivy nodded. "That's why I've never wanted to leave."

"Never?" Alfie asked, tipping his head to one side slightly. Ivy suddenly felt embarrassed. She surely seemed very provincial to some city-dweller. She wasn't sure what he did, but she remembered something being mentioned about lawyers and doctors. "You didn't want to see what else was out there?"

She flushed red. "I guess…" The Coke seemed to be sticking in her throat. Wasn't that exactly what she'd been asking herself? Whether she'd been wrong all along – wrong in thinking Jackson was 'the one' and wrong in thinking that this place was perfect for her and wrong in thinking that her future was—

"Sorry," she said, standing up quickly. "I'd better go. Thanks for the drink." She didn't meet his eyes as she reached for the door. She knew she was being ridiculous, but she couldn't answer his question, and it hurt to even think about it. She didn't want to cry in front of this handsome stranger who made her stomach flip and her heart race. That was better saved for the privacy of her bedroom, with its stupid purple walls.

"Wait, please, crap, look—" Her hand had only just reached the door handle when she felt his hand on her arm, nearly knocking the glass bottle of Coke from her hand. "I'm sorry, I didn't mean to offend you. I just say the first thing that comes to my head and I don't think about it. Ivy—"

How many times had she said those very same

words herself? That she spoke without thinking, that she jumped in before even considering the consequences.

"It's fine," she said, not looking back at him in case the tears in her eyes were apparent. "Don't worry about it. I just need to go..."

"Please stay. Finish your drink, at least?" He tugged gently on her arm, and she found herself turning back to face him. He was a good foot taller than she was, and she had to tip her head back to look into those blue eyes, which were full of his apology.

"Please?"

She swallowed. Standing this close to him, his hand on her arm, the sun beating down on them, she just couldn't think straight. Her head was a maelstrom of emotions that she had not expected that day.

"Okay," she whispered, because she didn't want to make him feel bad, just because she wanted to burst into tears at a simple question.

She wasn't sure who moved first. She would replay the moment over and over in her mind later that night, torturing herself, trying to figure out if it was something she actively chased, or something she went along with.

Something she went along with very willingly.

He leant forwards, and she stood on tiptoes, and his full lips met hers in the secluded wildflower garden.

She forgot that she was waiting for Christi to get back. She forgot about her misery. She forgot that she didn't know much more about this man than his first name.

That kiss set off fireworks in her stomach stronger than any she had ever felt before. She dropped the nearly-empty bottle onto the grass, not even thinking about the chance it might break, and wrapped her arms around his neck. He wrapped his around her waist, pulling her closer, tighter, and it felt so good to be wanted, especially by a man who looked like Alfie.

One of them opened the door and they tripped through it, falling back onto the king-size bed in the centre of the yurt.

"Is this..." Alfie asked, pulling away for a moment, his pupils wide and his breath ragged.

Ivy nodded. She didn't want to think, or talk. She just wanted to feel good, and forget everything that was hurting her heart.

CHAPTER ELEVEN

The excitement and thrill of the moment swept her along, and she didn't stop to think until the inevitable awkwardness hit.

Well, he didn't seem awkward, Ivy noticed as she pulled the duvet tightly around herself. In fact, she thought he'd fallen straight to sleep. Her heart raced as she watched his muscular chest rising and falling. He really was a beautiful man. His blond hair fell in front of his eyes, and she could picture their sparkling blue depths, even though they were closed.

What have I done? The question whirled around her mind as she contemplated her options: stay here in this naked man's bed, wake him up, or just sneak away.

The last seemed the least embarrassing, and so she slowly slid herself from the bed, finding her scattered clothes on the floor as she did so.

What have I done?

She had never slept with anyone but Jackson before. Never had a one-night stand. She couldn't even blame this on alcohol – because she'd not touched a drop, and Alfie had barely sipped his beer before…

Passion had never taken over her like that before. She'd been with Jackson for so long, and she had to admit that the exciting, can't-keep-your-hands-off-each-other phase of the relationship had faded long ago.

And before him, there was no one. He was her first, her only…until now.

Until a random Wednesday afternoon, in a luxury wooden yurt surrounded by wildflowers.

She pulled on her jeans, anxious that he might wake up and that she might have to discuss what the hell had happened. His breathing seemed to stutter and she froze, wondering if she ought to just leave without getting properly dressed – but of course, she quickly dismissed that idea. Being seen half-naked on the campsite would be far more embarrassing than having to have a conversation with the man she had just slept with.

Well, slightly more embarrassing.

Alfie rolled over and continued to sleep, and Ivy rushed to pull her t-shirt over her head, stuffing her bra in her pocket rather than bothering to put it on.

I don't even know his last name.

It was the most un-Ivy thing she thought she had ever done, and she didn't know how to feel about it. All she wanted to do was go home, where she could mentally dissect this without needing to worry about being interrupted by the man in question.

And then there was a knock on the door, and Alfie rolled over, his bright blue eyes very much open.

He grinned at her, and her heart fluttered in spite of itself.

"Alfie?" The voice was very definitely Christi's, and Ivy groaned internally. "Sorry to bother you. But have you seen my friend Ivy? You know, the one who delivered the cheese that time?"

Alfie's grin grew wider and Ivy cringed. She wasn't sure she wanted to be 'the girl who delivered the cheese'. Not when he was looking at her like that, and she knew full well he was naked under that duvet.

"I'm sure it's her car out here, but I can't see her anywhere!" Christi continued.

Alfie opened his mouth, and Ivy shook her head violently. She couldn't be found like this. She didn't know what she would say.

"I did see her," Alfie called out, and Ivy held her breath. "Told her you had gone into town. Think she went for a walk."

There was silence on the other side of the door, and Ivy waited, hoping Christi would leave so she could sneak out of there.

Alfie winked at her, and her stupid heart flipped. She definitely needed to get out of there – before she changed her mind and wanted to stay.

"Oh. Okay. I'll see if I can see her. Thanks."

The sound of footsteps walking away from the yurt faded into the distance, and Ivy's heart began to return to its normal pace.

"Thanks," she said.

"No problem. If you don't want her to know you were here…"

"It's just…" Ivy swallowed. "It's complicated. Sorry."

Alfie sat up, the duvet dangerously close to revealing everything, and shrugged. "Hey. No worries. You're okay, yeah?"

She nodded. "Fine. I'd better run. But…thanks."

Thanks? she repeated to herself as she opened the door, checked to make sure no one was there, and slid out. What was she thanking him for? The bottle of coke? The mind-blowing sex? Lying about her being there?

What a ridiculous response.

Now, she just needed to make it to her car, and then

"Ivy!" She froze at the sound of her name. "There you are! I was wondering where you'd got to. Have you been here long?"

Ivy turned to see the smiling face of Christi King. "Hey, Christi," she said, struggling to find words. "Not long, no."

"Sorry, we had to go into town, sign something for the house. Aunt Olivia is out for the day, but they needed both of us to sign, so we had to abandon the place to Alfie for a bit. He said he saw you?"

Hoping her cheeks weren't as red as they felt, she nodded.

"Come and have a cup of tea," Christi said, waving her over. "If you've got time? I presume you're not delivering, since you've not got the van…"

"No, I've got a day off," Ivy said, and then regretted it. If she'd said she was working, she could have left instantly – but now there was no way she could do so without seeming very rude.

"Good, you've been working far too hard."

"You must be swamped here though," Ivy said, not wanting to sit down with Christi and end up admitting what had just happened. She didn't even know how she felt about it yet; she didn't need anyone else's opinions. "I thought you might need a hand, but I don't want to get in the way…"

"We've not got anyone arriving or leaving today, actually. And Oscar's on top of all the maintenance! I need a cup of tea, come on."

❖ ❖ ❖

Olivia's kitchen didn't feel as comforting as it

usually did. Ivy couldn't stop her heart from racing, or her mind from wondering whether Alfie was going to appear, whether Christi knew that something had happened between them, whether she'd done something terrible.

All she wanted was to go home and figure all this out alone.

But she couldn't be rude to Christi. Christi was her only friend, really. The only one who knew everything about her and Jackson. The only person that she talked to honestly, on a regular basis.

But she couldn't talk to her about this. Not now, anyway.

"How have you been?" Christi asked, the kettle whistling away in the background.

"Oh, you know. Keeping busy. It keeps my mind off…everything."

Christi nodded understandingly, carrying the teapot over to the table.

"That's good. Just don't… Don't overdo it, yeah? You look pretty exhausted…"

Ivy went to run a hand through her hair, worried what a mess it was, but then remembered she had plaited it that morning. At least Christi was a little more tactful than her father and didn't say how awful she looked.

"That's why Dad's insisted I have a day off," Ivy said, rolling her eyes. "But I'm fine, honestly. It's better if I keep busy."

Christi sipped her tea. "I get that. But you definitely should have a break every now and then. We're having a wine and cheese night next week, for all the campers and the locals too. Obviously, I was going to order the cheese from you," Christi said with a grin, "but you should come too. It'll be fun."

"I'll see what I've got on," Ivy said noncommittally. She wanted to ask why Alfie was back, how long he was staying, maybe even find out his last name. Having slept with him, she had a newfound curiosity about this mysterious man.

Would he be here for the wine and cheese night? And would that change whether or not she was willing to attend?

"Alfie suggested it," Christi said, as if she could read Ivy's mind. "I know it seems a bit pretentious, but I think he's probably right – people will like it." She grinned. "Besides, he couldn't stop going on about your cheese."

Ivy blushed, but she had to seize her moment. Christi had brought him up without any prompting – she couldn't waste the chance to ask her questions.

"Why is he back?" she asked, taking a sip of her tea and hoping she sounded unconcerned.

"Apparently his parents want to buy a holiday home in the area, and they've tasked him with finding one and doing all the groundwork. It looks like he's staying for the whole summer."

Ivy almost choked on her tea. "The whole summer? Can he just stop working for a whole summer to find a house?"

Christi laughed. "That's how the other half live, hey. He's a lawyer, like my brother – so I'm guessing money isn't an issue. Especially with that sports car." She rolled her eyes. "He said he can do some work down here too, remotely – although he might get a shock when he realises how slow the internet is here. I know I did when I moved down here."

Ivy gulped at her tea, giving herself a little time to

think. He was going to be here the whole summer? And she had just slept with him, without thinking it through at all? She had never had a one-night stand before, but perhaps this wasn't destined to be a one-night stand. Or maybe it was... And now her deliveries, and her visits to her friend Christi, would be really awkward.

"Is that not a waste? To rent out that beautiful yurt for the whole summer?" Ivy asked when she realised she had been silent for far too long. It was better that she was asking the questions. She didn't want to be answering them.

"He's paid upfront for the whole summer," Christi said with a shrug. "And it's a very good price too. He's clearly got money, and he's not penny-pinching about it."

Ivy scrunched her eyebrows for a moment. Hadn't he said he was getting mates' rates? Did he think he was getting some great deal? Or was he paying above the odds purposefully, because Christi was his friend's sister?

Either way, Ivy was pleased that Christi wasn't losing out, even if she didn't know how to think about the beautiful man staying so close for the next six weeks.

Christi moved the conversation on, and Ivy struggled to pay attention. Her mind kept wandering back to earlier in the day. What was Alfie doing now? What did he think about what had happened this afternoon? Did he think badly of her? Or was this just his normal life? Picking up girls wherever he went? She felt rather naive, considering her lack of experience in the world.

"...Oscar tells me that not every summer is like this, but considering both summers I've been here have been beautiful so far, it's hard to believe him!"

Ivy laughed along with Christi, and then made her

excuses and finally got back into her car. Her eyes darted up to the yurt before she drove away, but there was no sign of Alfie. Maybe he'd gone back to sleep. Maybe he was getting ready to romance some other unsuspecting small-town girl...

◆ ◆ ◆

When she finally got home, Ivy set about making lasagna from scratch. She was relieved that Dad was still out on the farm, because it gave her some time to think.

She needed to be doing something, though, and making the lasagna at least kept her busy.

She couldn't think back on the afternoon without blushing.

How had she had the courage to sleep with a man whose surname she still didn't know? A man better-looking than any she had met? A man who was not Jackson?

She shook her head as she chopped onions and garlic. She shouldn't be thinking of Jackson right now. Just because Jackson was the only man who had ever seen her naked before.

Things with Alfie had been different. Well, of course they had. They didn't know each other. It was all different and new and exciting...

She felt guilty even thinking it, but it had been exciting. Her body tingled at the very thought.

"It was a one-off," she told herself as she made the sauces. "A moment of weakness. An escape from the misery I've been feeling."

There was no reason for it to happen again. She wasn't that kind of girl. She was a long-term relationship sort of woman. Well, she had been. One single long-term relationship that was now over. Why was she beating herself up about this? They were both single, consenting adults. Well, she was single, at least. She hoped he was… She hadn't even thought to ask.

When Dad came in for dinner, she forced the topic from her mind and put a smile on her face.

"Something smells good," he said, rubbing his hands together. "But I hope you've not spent your whole day off cooking…"

Ivy shook her head. "No. I went for a drive. Saw Christi…"

"Excellent," Dad said, washing his hands in the sink. "I won't feel guilty about enjoying a delicious homemade dinner, then."

After pretending all evening that everything was fine, Ivy was exhausted. She would be pleased to go to work the next day, just to have something to do other than pretend. She went to bed early, but she couldn't sleep. Instead, she trawled social media, torturing herself by searching for Jackson. He'd never had a presence online when they were together. Always said that it was a waste of time. And yet, she wasn't totally shocked when she found a profile for him. Apparently, people changed.

She felt guilty as she looked at his profile picture that she had slept with another man. It didn't make any sense. He had left. He didn't want her anymore. But the guilt churned in her stomach anyway.

And then she scrolled down and saw photo after photo with 'Tanya' tagged, photos of them kissing, hugging, grinning inanely.

And guilt wasn't the feeling churning in her stomach any more.

CHAPTER TWELVE

Ivy spent the next week telling herself that she absolutely was not going to go to the cheese and wine evening at the campsite. She managed to avoid going over there at all, getting one of the farm hands to make the weekly delivery. Her dad was so pleased that she wasn't working herself into the ground, that he didn't seem to be bothered that she was handing work off to someone else, and he didn't ask why she couldn't make that delivery in particular.

Even if she had forgotten about the cheese and wine night, she wouldn't have done so for long, because Christi texted her on the Friday morning, with a cheery reminder.

Haven't seen you around this week! Don't forget cheese and wine tonight! Get a lift if you can, so you can drink. Aunt Olivia would be happy for you to crash here, if your dad can't pick you up – my room's empty. X

The text distracted her for the rest of the day, making her lose count of the change she was giving the customers in the shop more than once.

She wasn't going.

She wasn't going.

And if she did go, she definitely wasn't going to stay over.

Because if she did... Alfie might want to talk. Or

more than talk.

Or he might want nothing to do with her.

The options all seemed equally terrifying. The guilt she'd felt for sleeping with another man had evaporated when she had seen evidence of how loved up Jackson was, so soon after leaving her. But she still didn't know how to deal with this situation. How she should act. What she should be thinking – and what he was thinking.

Was this just his regular routine? A new girl every night? Things had escalated between them so quickly. And he certainly knew what he was doing. It seemed likely that it wasn't a rare occurrence for him.

And yet… Maybe he thought the same about her. She hadn't hesitated either – even though, before him, there had only ever been one man in her life.

Whatever he thought of her, her mind was too messed up to go to the wine and cheese night. And if she went and actually had a few glasses of wine – well, who knew what she'd end up saying.

Whether it was another text from Christi – *Please come! It'll be fun!* – or the thought of Alfie's sparkling eyes, Christi wasn't sure, but when she got home from the shop, she found herself asking her dad for a lift.

"Sure," he said with a smile. "Always happy to help."

"Thanks. It's just it's a wine and cheese evening, and if I drive…"

"It'll just be a cheesy evening," Dad said with a chuckle. "And I'm sure you get plenty of cheese here. What time do you want me to pick you up?"

Ivy hesitated. Here was Dad offering to come and get her whenever she wanted. But she knew he always went to bed early, since the cows required him to get up at the crack of dawn.

And Christi had said she could stay...

"There's a spare room," she said, forging ahead even though she wasn't convinced that this wasn't a terrible idea. "I think I'll just stay, if that's okay."

Maybe a night away from the room she had spent so much time in lately would help. It was beginning to feel a bit suffocating.

"You're twenty-five, love, you don't have to ask my permission to stay over at your friend's house." Dad laughed. "But if you change your mind, just give me a ring. I don't mind coming over and getting you."

She pulled him into a tight hug, holding on for just a moment too long. "Thanks, Dad," she said, inhaling the comforting smell of the soap he always used. "You're the best."

◆ ◆ ◆

The nerves grew in the pit of her stomach as they drove over to Salcombe, and she nearly told Dad to turn around on several occasions. But how would she explain to him that she had changed her mind? She certainly wasn't going to mention Alfie to him.

And she didn't even know herself if she wanted to go, or why she wanted to go. She just knew that she felt more interested in going to Sunset Shore Campsite's wine and cheese night than she had about anything in a long while. Since Jackson had left.

Since before that, possibly.

She knew Christi had ordered extra cheese in her delivery, but she brought some more just in case. It seemed like a good excuse to come, even though she was invited.

There were still several weeks left of summer. She

would have ended up seeing Alfie at some point, even if she hadn't come to the cheese and wine night, she told herself as she got out of the car.

"Have fun. And remember, just ring and I can pick you up. Don't rush back tomorrow, though – you're definitely owed another day off. Andy can do the deliveries."

Ivy grabbed the little overnight bag that she had packed from the back seat and shut the door firmly. She wasn't sure how keen Andy would be on doing the deliveries – he very definitely preferred working around the farm.

"Thanks, Dad. I'll see you tomorrow, yeah?"

The summer evening was warm, and the sky was still light. Ivy dumped her bag in the porch of Olivia's house, surprised that there seemed to be no one in, and made her way onto the field. Christi had set up a bar the previous summer, and that was where everyone was gathered tonight. The field was packed with campers and locals chatting and enjoying the summer sunshine. Ivy took in a deep breath of the warm air, her eyes darting around to try to spot Alfie.

"Ivy! You came. Here, have a glass," Christi said, handing her a glass of red wine. Ivy normally drank white, but she thought tonight that anything would do. She needed to settle the nerves in her stomach.

"Thanks for inviting me. I brought some more cheese, just in case," she said, holding up the paper bag in her other hand.

"You didn't have to do that."

"Are you sure it's all right for me to crash in your old room? I thought I'd have a drink, but I can get Dad to pick me up if not."

"Totally fine. I've already run it past Aunt Olivia. Tonight is going to be great. I'm so glad Alfie suggested that we do this."

Ivy felt her cheeks warm just at the mention of his name, and she hadn't even set eyes on him yet.

"Oscar's lighting the fire pit, there's marshmallows if you want them, and of course, a lot of cheese. Might be best to have the cheese first, actually," Christi said with a giggle, and Ivy wondered how much wine she'd already had. Not that she begrudged her friend. She worked hard, so why shouldn't she play hard?

Ivy found herself a seat on a log by the fire pit, glancing around to see who she recognised. There were plenty of locals, some whom she recognised from her school days, some from the deliveries, some from coming into the shop. She waved and smiled whenever anyone noticed her, but she felt rather alone.

Everyone was there with someone. Maybe she should have brought Dad. Although that would have been awkward if Alfie did appear. Maybe this was a mistake altogether. She sipped her wine and wondered how early she could bow out.

"Drinking alone?" a voice said, and Ivy turned to find the smiling face of Alfie looming above her.

"I–uh–" Why would the stupid words not come?

"I was only joking," he said, taking a seat on the log beside her. His thigh pressed against hers, and her whole body felt warm.

"I know," she said with a smile, rather worried that he would think she was offended by everything he said. When in truth, he just stopped her from being able to think straight.

"I'm glad you came," he said, sipping from his own

wineglass.

The warmth in her body grew hotter. "It was your idea, I hear," she said, proud of herself for putting a full sentence together.

"Well. I do really like cheese, and yours honestly is the best I've tasted. And this place is so beautiful, and I'm here for the summer..." He shrugged. "I just thought it might be nice. And bring a bit more attention to this place. Christi deserves it, she works so hard."

Ivy nodded. She was finding it increasingly hard to think up sensible conversation with his leg pressed against hers.

"She does. She's worked wonders here. They've bought a big house in the next village, did you know? They're doing it up, going to turn it into a B&B."

Alfie looked impressed. "I knew they'd bought a house, but I didn't realise it was such a business prospect. I just thought they were living there. Christi lived here before, didn't she?"

Ivy nodded. "With her aunt, yeah. I'm going to stay in her room tonight, so I can have a drink or two." She didn't know what had possessed her to say that out loud. Now she couldn't change her mind. She'd lost the option of ringing Dad and ending the night early.

Something about Alfie just seemed to make her want to stay.

"That's nice," he said, his eyes seeming to smoulder in the firelight, rather than sparkle.

"Yeah, it is. Christi's just so nice – and Olivia, and Oscar too." Ivy felt as though she had forgotten that they were surrounded by people. She was only interested in Alfie, and he only seemed interested in her. It made her feel...something that wasn't misery, anyway.

"They seem very happy."

"They deserve to be," Ivy said, sipping her wine. Did she not deserve to be happy? Her own words filled her mind. Had she done something to deserve Jackson walking out on her after so many years?

She looked dazedly into the firelight for a few moments, until Alfie disturbed her reverie in a low voice. "I'm glad you're okay... After the other day. It was all a bit...unexpected."

Ivy nearly choked on her wine. "You can say that again."

"Not in a bad way," Alfie said hurriedly, and when she looked up at him, his boyish face was full of worry. She had a strong desire to kiss him, and although she did not give in to it, the notion itself surprised her.

"That's good," she said in a whisper. She had wondered whether he was regretting their dalliance, and it was a relief to hear that he wasn't.

"It's just...you ran away. And I wanted to make sure..."

Ivy smiled. She wasn't going to give in and kiss him, but she could at least reassure him that everything was okay. Well, as okay as it could be. She placed a hand lightly on his knee, surprising herself a little. "It's fine. You...you're pretty incredible. I'm just in a weird place right now, that's all. I'm sorry."

She didn't remove her hand from his knee, and then he covered it with his own. She briefly considered how this would look if anyone who knew her could see, but decided she didn't care enough to remove it. It felt too good.

"You don't have to apologise," Alfie said, their eyes meeting. "But if you want to talk about it..."

Ivy laughed, and then realised that was quite an odd reaction, and reined it in. "Thank you. I don't think I want to talk about it. Not tonight, anyway. It's a beautiful evening. I don't want to ruin it."

He held her gaze for too long, and she nearly, so nearly gave in to the urge to press her lips to his. Her mind was screaming at her to do it. Why couldn't she have a fling? It didn't have to mean anything. People did it all the time. But the rational side of her brain said that it would be awkward, and that this wasn't her, and that the only serious relationship in her life had so recently ended. It wasn't the time to go and get her heart broken by some blond-haired god.

"We should go and get some cheese," she said eventually, breaking the moment between them. "Before it's all gone." Alfie nodded, and beamed, and Ivy let out a sigh of relief. Things weren't particularly awkward. He wasn't embarrassed that something had happened between them. She could be here, and enjoy herself, and it didn't have to mean she was going to end up in his bed…

CHAPTER THIRTEEN

"So what's going on with you two?" Christi asked with a grin, taking a seat next to Ivy by the fire.

Alfie hadn't been gone long – he'd gone to get some more wine – and Ivy was amazed at how quickly Christi had made a beeline for her. They had obviously not been as subtle as they had thought.

"What do you mean?" Ivy asked, wondering if there was any chance that the dusky sky was hiding her flushed cheeks.

Christi laughed. "You know exactly what I mean. You and Alfie – you can't keep your eyes off each other."

Ivy gulped the end of the wine to give herself a moment to think.

"Don't think I haven't seen you and Oscar all over each other by the bar all night," Ivy said, wondering if the best defence was to go on the offensive.

Christi smirked. "There's just one issue there."

"Oh?" Ivy said, her eyes wide. Part of her wanted Alfie to come back quickly to rescue her. But part of her knew that Christi's questioning would only increase upon Alfie's return.

"Oscar and I are a couple. You and Alfie, as far as I know, are not."

Ivy's stomach sank. "Oh. Well. Yeah…"

Christi elbowed her, nearly sloshing the end of Ivy's

own wine – white this time – everywhere. "Relax, I'm just winding you up. He's hot, you're hot. He's single, you're single."

Sure that her cheeks were now burning red, Ivy looked to the floor, trying to think of an answer. She'd never been part of jokes about flirting and crushes and one-night stands because she'd been with Jackson her entire adult life. They had jokes about how they'd be getting married, having children, and settling down…

Jokes that made Ivy feel miserable to think about now.

At the sound of footsteps, Ivy looked up, and there was Alfie, a permanent smile on his face, a glass of wine in each hand.

"Talk of the devil…" Christi said, slurring slightly. "Now, I know you're my brother's friend, and I do hold that against you," she said with a giggle. "But you seem like a decent guy. So make sure you treat my Ivy right."

Ivy thought she might die of embarrassment. But Alfie simply laughed, handed Ivy a glass of wine to replace her now-empty one, and assured Christi that he had only the very best intentions.

And then he gave Ivy a smouldering look that sent her insides swirling. How did he do that?

"There you are," a deep masculine voice said, and Oscar joined their little gathering. Christi threw her arms around him, and he steadied her and laughed. "I think you might have had one too many – or just not enough cheese. Come on, time for bed."

"Oooh," Christi said in a suggestive tone, before allowing Oscar to lead her away. "Good night, Alfie, Ivy. Don't do anything I wouldn't do!"

"I might just die of embarrassment right now," Ivy

said, hiding her head in her hands. "I've never seen Christi drunk."

Alfie laughed. "She's just letting loose. It's funny. Besides, Oscar is sober, he'll get her home and make sure she drinks some water, I'm sure."

Ivy nodded and dared to look at him. He was almost even more handsome now that the sun had set, and the orange glow of the fire lit up his face. She didn't know if it was the wine, Christi's words, or just being here with him, but she really, really wanted to kiss him.

"You know," he said, his tongue darting out to wet his lips, "I've got that king-size bed. It's too big for just me..."

Ivy's heart pounded. She'd told herself it was a one-off. That it was a bad idea. But right now, he didn't seem like such a bad idea. Like Christi had said, they were both single. Who were they harming?

"If you wanted to come back...." He ran a hand through his hair. "It's up to you." Ivy swallowed, her throat suddenly very dry, and then she nodded. She leaned forwards, finally giving in to the desire that had been building within her all evening, and pressed her lips to his. She could taste the wine, the marshmallows they had toasted on the fire, and somehow she didn't care about anything other than him in that moment. Not the people watching. Not her broken heart. Not the fact that she didn't do this sort of thing, and it might lead to heartbreak again, and that she didn't know this man.

She had thought she knew Jackson. But boy, had she been wrong. And this wasn't forever. This wasn't love.

And just maybe a summer fling would be enough to make her heart forget it was broken. To let it start to move on.

◆ ◆ ◆

The next morning was not as awkward as the last time. Maybe because they had actually fallen asleep together, and woken up together, entangled in the bed covers and each other's arms. She still felt uncomfortable at him seeing her naked, and she had a bit of a hangover, but it was a bit more expected than the previous time.

And as she'd planned to stay the night at Olivia's, she did at least have a toothbrush and a spare change of clothes, so she didn't feel totally awful.

"I was meant to be getting up early this morning to look at houses for my parents," Alfie said, glancing at his watch. "But I think that boat has sailed."

Ivy wondered if he actually had a boat. From what Christi said, it sounded like he had money. And to be able to take the entire summer off... Well, clearly money wasn't a huge concern, anyway. They came from different worlds, but she supposed that didn't matter too much for a summer fling.

"I've actually got the day off," she said, relieved that Dad had suggested it.

"How about I take you for a coffee then? You can give me the lowdown on the best places to buy, since you're an expert on this area."

Ivy blushed. She hadn't been meaning to hint that they should spend the day together, and part of her wondered if that was really what you did with a casual fling.

But the sun was shining, she had an empty day ahead of her, and Alfie made her want to smile.

"Go on then. I haven't got my car, though..."

"I've got mine, don't worry."

Ivy raised an eyebrow. "That sports car? You're not worried about scratching it on the lanes?"

Alfie laughed. "I'm not as precious as Anthony is about his car, don't worry. You tell me where to go, and I'll drive there. As long as they do strong coffee…"

"Oh, I've got the perfect place," Ivy said, feeling her face light up. "You'll love it." On such a lovely day, and with someone who didn't live near the sea, the only place that made sense was somewhere overlooking the ocean. She couldn't quite bring herself to go on the beach just yet, thanks to the memories it brought back, but a hotel overlooking the sea would surely be okay.

On their way out of the yurt, they ran straight into Olivia – who had a knowing grin on her face.

"Good morning, Alfie, Ivy," she said. "I did wonder where you had got to!"

Ivy blushed, and was grateful when Olivia carried on about her business, not stopping to interrogate them. She was sure that Christi would want to know more, as soon as Olivia mentioned where Ivy had spent the night, but that was an issue for another time. Alfie grabbed her hand, something he seemed to do without even thinking about it, and she giggled as she was pulled towards the car.

◆ ◆ ◆

The village of Hope Cove wasn't somewhere Ivy visited regularly, but every time she did, she remembered how much she loved it. As Alfie's fancy car wound through the narrow lanes, Ivy enjoyed the warmth of the sun on her face. And then they rounded the corner, and the beach nestled in the cove came into view, and Ivy's heart ached a little.

She missed the beach. She hadn't been able to bring herself to go since Jackson had broken her heart on Blackpool Sands more than two months earlier. It was proving to be another beautiful summer, and yet she'd not been able to sink her toes into the warm sand, or dip in the sea.

"Wow, it is beautiful," Alfie said, breaking her miserable train of thought. "Maybe I should see if there are any houses for sale around here. My parents would love it."

Ivy directed him to the car park of 'Cove Crest Inn', a little hotel overlooking the beach. "It's pretty pricey round here," she said as he parked. "But I guess if that's not an issue…"

They were shown to the terrace and ordered coffee. Ivy took a seat on a wicker sofa, presuming Alfie would sit in the chair opposite, but he sat down beside her, his knee pressed against hers.

"Do your parents have any links down here then?" Ivy asked when their coffees were brought out. The sun sparkled on the sea, and she found herself feeling jealous of the family swimming in the ocean. Maybe it wouldn't be too painful to go back to the beach. Not Blackpool Sands yet, but one of the many beautiful beaches in the area. They had always made her feel like everything was right with the world before. The beach was where she felt closest to her mum, and she missed it.

"Not really," he said. "We came down on holiday as kids, like I think most people in the UK do at some point…"

"Were you a 'tents in the rain and wind' kind of family? Or luxury hotels?" she asked with a grin.

Alfie shaded his eyes from the sun and laughed.

"Luxury hotels, although I don't know where you got that idea from..."

"Oh, I don't know. Sports car, hunting down a holiday home in Hope Cove, the fact that you can take a whole summer off your job without ending up homeless..."

"Dad ran a big tech business, until he retired," Alfie said. "But I'm a self-made man – and I really do work hard as a lawyer, when I'm not in Devon on summer errands for my parents..."

His smile was easy, and when he leaned forward to put his cup back on the little glass coffee table, he rested his other hand on her knee. Sparks flew from the point of contact, and for a moment Ivy forgot what she was saying.

"I'm sure you do," she said. "Do your parents live near you?" she asked, trying desperately to remember where it was Alfie lived. She knew it was a city... but beyond that, her memory failed her. She had been rather too distracted by his disarming good looks and charm every time they had met to remember details.

He shook his head. "They're near London, so not too far – but they want somewhere more rural. And when they said they needed someone to scout out places down here...well, I was keen to come back. So I offered." The look in his eyes sent a shiver down her spine that she tried to ignore.

He hadn't been keen to come back to see her. That would be ridiculous. They'd met so briefly that first time. And Ivy had been in a daze about Jackson. No, he'd been attracted to the beautiful location. And who wouldn't want to spend the whole summer in Devon?

Ivy wanted to spend her entire life there. She

understood the attraction.

"It's a bit of a trek, down here from Oxford," he said, and she was very pleased that he had mentioned his home town before she had to ask. "So it only really made sense to stay for the whole summer."

"Oh, of course," Ivy said with a giggle. "The only logical option."

"Would you prefer I chose a house and left next week?" he asked with raised eyebrows.

Without thinking, she reached out and put her hand over his on her knee. She knew this was just for the summer. She knew there were no strings. But she still didn't like to think of him leaving suddenly.

"No. You should stay. Devon is beautiful."

"Devon isn't the only beautiful reason to spend the summer…" he said, and although the words were cheesy, they sent a tingle through her body.

"You are a real smooth talker," she said, her cheeks blushing. Part of her wanted to ask if he was like this everywhere he went – a girl in every port, so to speak.

But then she told herself it didn't matter. And asking would only ruin things.

"Not too cheesy?" he asked with a grin.

She laughed. "Not too much."

"Well, you know how much I like cheese…" he said. She cracked up at the pun, and when he pulled her in for a kiss on the sun-drenched terrace, her heart felt full.

CHAPTER FOURTEEN

Although work continued to fill her days, Ivy found herself at Sunset Shore Campsite on several of the evenings the following week. Seeing Alfie didn't erase her heartache, but it made it easier to ignore. And although burning the candle at both ends was exhausting, it was far better than crying herself to sleep at night.

She still had no idea where her life was going, but she could only hope that it would all work out in the end.

For now, not crying was a win.

As she expected, when she delivered to the campsite two days after the wine and cheese night, it was not Alfie who greeted her, but Christi, with a determined grin on her face.

"The kettle's already on," she said. "I saw your van coming up the hill. And no excuses about needing to get away."

Ivy's cheeks flushed red, but she followed her friend inside, noticing immediately that Alfie's sports car was not parked in the drive. She supposed he was out looking for houses, since that was the reason he was spending the summer.

He wasn't her boyfriend. She didn't expect to know where he was. And that was quite freeing, really – because with Jackson, she had expected to know, and yet often hadn't.

At least with this, they both knew where they stood.

"I knew there was something going on between you and Alfie!" Christi said the second the front door was closed.

Ivy groaned. "Christi… I'm no good at conversations like this."

"I know I'd had a couple of drinks the other night…"

Ivy giggled. It was certainly more than a couple.

"But I knew there was something between you." Ivy's cheeks felt even hotter, and she was pleased when Christi put the tea on the table, so she had something to do with her hands. "Hey," Christi said. "No judgment from me. He's cute, if you like guys like that…"

Ivy wasn't sure what straight woman *wouldn't* like a guy like Alfie. He was beautiful, and funny, and sweet, and the chemistry between them was like nothing she had ever known before.

Her cheeks felt like they might explode at that thought. That was the problem with having been with the same man for so many years – she wasn't used to flings and answering questions and people not just knowing who she was with.

Jackson and Ivy. Their names had been intertwined for so long, it was hard for Ivy to hear them separately.

It was something she was slowly getting used to.

"Are you happy?" Christi asked, concern colouring her features. "You know he's only here for the summer, right? He's a nice guy, don't get me wrong – probably the best of any of my brothers' friends. But I don't want to be the reason you get hurt, not after…everything."

Ivy sipped her tea. "I'm a grown-up, Christi. It's my responsibility to make sure I don't get hurt, don't worry. And I know he's only here for the summer. It's just... fun. A summer fling. It's about time I had one, don't you think?"

Christi nodded slowly. "If he hurts you, he'll have me to answer to."

Warmth flooded through Ivy at the care her friend had for her. It made her feel a little less alone.

"Jackson," she began, forcing the unspeakable name out, "really hurt me. Made me question everything. And I'm still not sure what I want or where my life is going. But for this summer... I'm going to enjoy myself."

◆ ◆ ◆

Half of the summer seemed to be gone in the blink of an eye. Ivy would wake up more often than not in the sunny circular wooden yurt, wrapped up in Alfie's strong arms. Then she'd have to rush home to get the deliveries ready, or straight to the shop in town. She was always almost late – and she wasn't sure her dad was buying the fact that she was spending several nights a week at Christi and Oscar's.

Well, it wasn't entirely a lie. After all, they did run the campsite with Olivia. And that was where she was.

Either way, her dad seemed pleased that she wasn't overtly miserable any more – even if he did raise his concerns more than once that she was racing around and never having a moment of downtime.

Ivy didn't want downtime, though. Downtime meant that she sat and thought about where her life was heading and what Jackson was doing right now and where everything had gone wrong...

It was much better to work and see Alfie and enjoy the beautiful sunshine, and not stop to ruminate.

All her deep, dark worries for the future could wait until the autumn.

"I think you work harder than I do," Alfie said one morning, as the rising sun filtered through a gap in the curtains. "You're up at the crack of dawn and you never stop. I thought I did long hours!"

"I'm sure you're paid far more for them," she said as she buttoned up her shirt and plaited her hair deftly in the mirror. "But it's a small family business, and there's always so much to do. When I don't have to get back home to get the stock before I make deliveries, it's not quite as long…"

Alfie screwed up his face. "I don't want you to be overdoing it because you're coming here…"

Ivy shook her head, and bent down to press a kiss to his warm, pink lips without even thinking about it. Things with Alfie often seemed to be like that – easy. Effortless. It was a nice change of pace.

"I didn't mean that. I'm happy to get up a bit earlier – if you're happy to have me here."

He grinned. "I think you know that I am," he said, reaching out and pulling her back into bed for a proper kiss. "You could always be late…"

She laughed and wriggled from his grasp. "I'm already late, I'm afraid. But I'm free tonight…"

There was always a moment of doubt, that niggling fear that someone as handsome as Alfie wouldn't want to spend time with her any more. That the enthusiasm was all one-sided.

But the beam on his face told her otherwise, and sent her stomach somersaulting.

CHAPTER FIFTEEN

Work, spending time with Christi, and seeing Alfie, stopped Ivy from slipping into the misery that had surrounded her in the first days after Jackson left. She forced herself not to think of him, or the time that she had wasted with him. She didn't look him up on social media, and when she spotted his parents, she avoided them.

But on a Monday morning in August, when she had spent the night at home and was getting ready to head into Kingsbridge to open up the dairy shop, the envelope was pushed through the letterbox – and all the questions she had been pushing away flooded back into her head.

It was a heavy cream envelope, with the farmhouse address written in calligraphy, and it was addressed to Miss Ivy Thompson and Mr Jackson Shaw.

That was the first thing to throw her off her stride that morning. Whoever had sent this didn't know they had broken up. Ivy hadn't exactly announced it anywhere, but she presumed anyone who knew her well enough to send a letter would have heard through some mutual acquaintance.

But apparently not.

Already running late, she shoved it into her handbag and drove to work, trying to ignore the stabbing in her heart at the sight of their names together.

How many times before had she seen their names together and smiled? Or imagined them entwined more permanently: Mr and Mrs Shaw. Ivy and Jackson Shaw.

Just thinking about the assumptions she had made for years hurt. She was glad when she got to work that there was a customer waiting for her to open up. At least that kept her busy. Then, when she got five minutes, she checked her phone – and a text from Alfie made her smile, and improved the day a little.

Just saw the most amazing house in Hope Cove. You can see the sea from the garden, and it made me think of you. Fancy going out for a drink tonight? X

He signed his messages with kisses as though he didn't think anything of it – and he probably didn't. He was charming and flirtatious and friendly with everyone, and Ivy had to remind herself not to read too much into it. She had never had a fling before, and so it was very easy to slip into a relationship mentality. That would only lead to disaster. She was having so much fun with Alfie – and she needed to keep that in mind.

A drink sounded like fun. And a bit like a date, which sent a thrill through her body. And then they would presumably go back to his place – well, his yurt, anyway.

If only she had the following day off. But still, it was worth the ridiculously early start to the day.

Sounds great. I'll come over after work – there's some nice pubs in Salcombe, and we could walk back if we don't want to drive. She debated adding a kiss to the end herself, as she always did. She couldn't be quite as free and easy as him, but surely he'd think she was cold and rude if she didn't add one, since he always did? Self-consciously she added one on the end and pressed send, pleased to have something to look forward to.

As the bell above the shop dinged to alert her to another customer, she slid her phone back into her bag, and felt the thick envelope against her fingertips.

The next time the shop was empty she opened it, and a heavyweight cream card with purple flowers around the edges fell out onto the countertop.

Casey and Elijah request the presence of Ivy and Jackson to celebrate their marriage on November 1st at 12.30pm.

Casey was getting married?

Ivy left the card on the table and reread it several times without picking it up. The hotel's address was listed, and a contact number to RSVP, but the only bits she could focus on were her and Jackson's names, and that word: marriage.

She and Casey had been close friends at secondary school. They'd stayed in touch when Casey had gone off to uni in Bath, too – although when her parents had left Devon, they'd not seen each other very often. Opportunities had been few and far between.

Ivy hadn't even known she was engaged, let alone getting married.

She knew she should be happy for her friend, and grateful for an invite, considering they hadn't spoken much in the last couple of years.

Clearly not at all in recent months, since she knew nothing about the break up of Ivy and Jackson's relationship.

Suddenly, all the worries that she had been pushing to the back of her mind broke free. She had thought that she would be the one getting married but now she was just a twenty-five-year-old living at home with her dad, having a casual fling with a gorgeous guy who would soon disappear and forget that she ever existed.

She had no plans. She would continue to work in this shop and deliver milk and cheese and butter and whatever else they decided to make to local clients. She would live with her dad and sleep in her stupid purple room and before she knew it she would be thirty and nothing would have changed.

She'd always thought she'd be married and have children before she hit twenty-five. She'd thought everything would work out with Jackson. She'd thought her life was set.

Everything with Alfie the past few weeks had been a distraction. A wonderful, exciting distraction. But it didn't change the burning mess her life had become. When Alfie left, he would return to an incredible career and some amazing flat in Oxford.

And where would she be?

Here. Alone. With nothing to work towards and no plans for the future.

As another customer opened the door, she swiped away tears furiously and shoved the stupid invitation back in her bag.

There was no way she was going alone, to show all her school friends what a failure she was.

But the invitation would not stop playing on her mind.

She cancelled her drink with Alfie before she got in her car to drive home. Her head was just not in it, no matter how much she had been looking forward to it.

Sorry, something's come up, can we take a rain check on that drink? X

The reply beeped through while she was driving, and she checked it as soon as she pulled up at the farmhouse.

Of course. See you soon x

A prompt response, and no expectations, no pressure, no questions. It was everything a summer fling should be.

And yet it didn't make her feel any better.

She set to work cooking a bolognese once she got in, feeling bad for abandoning her dad to freezer meals so often lately. He came in from the farm not long after, with a genuine smile on his face at seeing her there. That only made her feel more guilty.

"Hello, love," he said, washing his hands in the sink. "That smells good!"

"It won't be ready for another half an hour I'm afraid," Ivy said, stirring the meat so it wouldn't stick. "I didn't plan ahead, only got started when I got home."

"No rush. I'm going to take a quick shower anyway."

Ivy had far too much time to think in the peace and quiet of the kitchen. She wondered what she would be doing now, if Jackson *had* proposed like she'd expected him to. She wouldn't have met Alfie, that was for sure – or if she had, it would have been a quick hello, and maybe a joke with Christi about how handsome he was, and then she would have forgotten all about him.

They might have set a date. Have been planning a big celebration. Probably for the following summer, because Ivy had always dreamed of a summer wedding, with photos taken on the beach. They would surely have moved in together, if they were engaged.

She would have known where her life was heading.

She was so lost in her thoughts that she didn't even

notice her dad coming back into the kitchen and taking a seat at the table.

"You've been very busy lately, love," he said, making her jump.

She turned to face him. "I know. I'm sorry, Dad, I don't mean to leave you alone so often…"

Dad shook his head. "It wasn't a criticism. It's nice to see you out and about, seeing your friends."

Guilt ate away at her for the lies she had told in order to go and see Alfie, but she pushed it down. It was only a white lie. It wasn't done to hurt Dad – just to avoid an awkward discussion.

"Just don't overdo it, eh? You can't be getting enough sleep, dashing all over the place like that!"

Her cheeks flamed red and she turned back to put the pasta on to boil.

"It's all good, Dad," she said, even though inside, she didn't feel all good at all.

She felt like, once again, the rug had been pulled from under her.

It wasn't that she was still devastated about Jackson, although she tried not to think about him, as it was still upsetting. She missed him, which was particularly galling considering he'd left her for another woman.

No, it was the loss of the life she had been working towards, the path she had thought she was following, that was really getting to her right now.

And her school friend getting married only highlighted that.

"How are you doing?" Dad asked over dinner. It was a question that Ivy didn't truthfully know the answer to. She'd thought that she was fine, before that envelope.

She'd thought that it would all work out, that she would get things back on track, that it didn't matter how she spent the summer, she would figure out a new path once the autumn rolled around.

"I..." She paused, twirled some spaghetti on her fork, and tried to decide how much she wanted to share. She certainly didn't want to start crying. Dad was no good with emotions. And talking about feelings...well, that wasn't his strong suit either. But she couldn't just sit there and ignore the maelstrom of confusing thoughts that filled her head.

"I was invited to a wedding today," she said. "Do you remember Casey, from school?" Dad nodded. "She sent an invitation. To me and Jackson..."

"Oh," Dad said, pausing in lifting his fork to his mouth.

"It's not just that," Ivy said, wanting to move the conversation along from Jackson. "I guess...it reminds me I'm not really going anywhere."

Dad frowned. "Do you want to go somewhere?"

Ivy shook her head. "I don't think so. I mean...in life. I still live at home, I'm single, I don't have any big plan I'm working towards..."

"You're young, love," Dad said, his eyes crinkling into a smile. "It will all work out."

Ivy sighed. "Yeah. I thought that. But I thought things were going to work out perfectly with Jackson, and they haven't. And now... I guess I just feel a bit of a failure."

"You are anything but, Ivy Thompson. You've built up the dairy so that it's profitable and can support us both! You know I wouldn't have done the deliveries and the shop without you. And that none of it runs the same when you're not there."

Ivy managed a weak smile. "Thanks, Dad. And I do love living here with you…"

"And I love having you here. But I don't expect you to stay here forever, don't worry," he said with a grin.

"I don't want to live with strangers," Ivy said with a sigh. "But affording rent on my own…"

"It's time I gave you a pay rise," Dad said.

"No, Dad, that's not why I'm saying this, honest. You pay me plenty. You need money for you, too, and to put back into the farm. Maybe I'll look into some places I can afford on my own, or will be able to if I save up. Maybe that will feel like a good goal…"

"I know it feels like everyone else is racing ahead with their lives," Dad said. "But you shouldn't compare yourself to anyone else. You are you, and as long as you are happy and healthy, nothing else matters."

The problem was, Ivy reflected in her own bed that night, that she wasn't sure she was happy. It wasn't that she wanted someone else's life – she didn't pine after Christi's campsite or Casey's husband. She just wanted to be where she had always thought she would be by this point in her life. She didn't want to feel like a failure.

She wasn't even sure it was about Jackson any more. She missed him, and she was still hurt that he had left like that, but occasionally she could see that it might have been for the best.

She had realised that she couldn't remember the last time things had been fun with Jackson.

That she had spent years walking on eggshells, not knowing whether he was going to respond, whether she was going to see him, what his mood would be like.

She knew it didn't make sense to compare; that the

two relationships, if she could even use that word, were totally different. But the easy, joyful days and nights she had spent with Alfie only made it more obvious what hard work things had been with Jackson in the later years.

And maybe the earlier ones, too. It was so hard to know what she had been viewing with rose-tinted glasses, because it was the past and because everyone had said what a perfect couple they were.

She'd told herself for years that they were perfect for each other. Soul mates.

She'd never thought that she would be proven so wrong.

CHAPTER SIXTEEN

"Sorry about the other night," Ivy said as they sat down in a little bar in Salcombe, overlooking the water.

"It's no problem. I caught up on some work – I have not been as diligent as I should have been lately," Alfie said with his usual grin.

"Getting easily distracted?" Ivy asked with a smile.

"Very much so. By you in the evenings, and by the beautiful weather in the daytime. I've been looking at houses some of the time, but sitting down at my laptop to work is not appealing when I could be swimming in the sea whenever I'm free."

Ivy's blush from the compliments had not died down by the time he looked at her, waiting for some sort of response.

"I can't blame you, although some of us have to work, no matter how beautiful the weather and inviting the sea." She missed the beach. Most summers, she practically lived down there in her spare time, even when the weather wasn't as wonderful as it was this year. Maybe it wouldn't be too painful to go down one day after work, to wash away the stress and the grime of the day.

"Where have you been swimming?" she asked.

"I've been to both beaches in Salcombe, and then a couple Olivia recommended to me – one over in Thurlestone, I think it's called, and one just around the corner from it."

Ivy nodded. "That'll be South Milton Sands. All very good choices. You should try Torcross, too, although be careful, the beach shelves really quickly, so it's pretty deep." Her eyes darted to the strong muscles framed by his short-sleeved shirt. "Although I'm guessing you're a pretty strong swimmer."

She blushed furiously when she realised she had said that out loud. Just because she was sleeping with the guy didn't mean she ought to be casually commenting on his physique.

"I think I do okay," Alfie said with a laugh. "But I was always told not to swim alone, and I've been breaking that rule. You should come with me sometime."

"Yeah, maybe," Ivy said, her stomach churning slightly. There was no reason that anything bad would happen if she went to the beach with Alfie, but her mind couldn't quite comprehend that.

"Any luck with finding a house for your parents?" Ivy asked, keen to change the subject.

"There are a few contenders. I'm going to send them pictures and see what they want me to do next."

"And then..." Ivy said, biting her bottom lip.

"Yeah," Alfie said, the smile dropping off his face for a rare moment. "I'll be heading back to Oxford. I've got a big case starting on the third of September, so I've got to be home by then at the latest."

The third of September. It really wasn't very far away. They were already in August. And of course, he might find a house sooner and decide it wasn't worth sticking around for the rest of the summer.

Ivy swallowed a lump in her throat and took a sip of wine to hide the sadness that had washed over her. This was not news. They might not have discussed the ins and outs of whatever was going on between them, but she had always known it was temporary. That was the excitement of it.

But that didn't mean she wouldn't be sad when it ended.

"It's been an amazing summer," Alfie said, raising his bottle of beer in a toast to her. "I hope you know that."

Ivy smiled softly. "Even though I keep distracting you from your work?"

Alfie grinned, and it lit up his whole face. "Especially because you keep distracting me from my work."

When she woke up the next day wrapped in his arms, she tried to push all her worries about the future away. She had maybe three weeks of fun left, before she would be alone again, and there would be plenty of time to worry about what the future held.

She worried, as she watched him sleeping for a few moments before she really had to get up, that she'd let herself get too attached to Alfie. That she wasn't cut out for a fling, for a summer of fun – that deep down, she was only built for serious relationships.

The conversation about the temporary nature of their relationship hadn't really been had in so many words – but he'd made it clear he was leaving at the end of the summer, so that was that.

She'd thought she was happy about that. That it was the perfect situation.

But now the end of the summer looked even bleaker than it normally did.

She slipped away while he was still sleeping. There was no reason both of them needed to be up at the crack of dawn.

Her phone started to ring when she reached the main road, but she ignored it. She could ring whoever it was back when she got home. Then it rang again, and she pulled off into lay-by. If someone was so desperate to get hold of her before seven in the morning, it was surely urgent.

"Hello?"

"Ivy, it's Andy," the urgent voice on the other end of the line said. Ivy frowned. She couldn't remember Andy their farmhand ever ringing her. She hadn't even known he had her number. He always dealt with Dad about anything to do with the farm.

"Oh, hi. What's up?"

"There's been an accident," he said, and Ivy's blood ran cold.

"What—"

"Your dad. He's fallen off a wall. I don't know all the details, he was on the floor when I got here. He's gone to Torbay hospital, in the ambulance."

"Is-was-" Ivy couldn't get the words out. Her hands were shaking, her heart racing, and she wanted someone to take over in this terrifying situation.

"He was conscious, when they left," he said.

"Okay. Okay. I'll drive there now," Ivy said, already starting the engine. "Can you ring the usual delivery customers, explain I won't be able to deliver today?" she asked. It was a struggle to stay calm, to tell herself everything would be all right, and focusing on the mundane, everyday tasks went someway to helping her in that.

"I'll sort it all, don't worry. Just let me know how he's doing, yeah? And if you need anything driving down, just call."

"Thanks, Andy," Ivy said, feeling tearful.

She drove in silence all the way to the hospital. It was certainly one of the downsides of living so rurally – the nearest hospitals were nearly an hour away. Was Dad there yet? Was he okay? Were they able to help him?

It felt like the longest journey in the world. She wished she'd asked more details from Andy, because she had no idea what he was going to be like when she got there. What wall had he fallen from? And how badly was he hurt? Enough that an ambulance was needed. If he was conscious when they left, did that mean he'd been unconscious at some point?

He was all she had, and she was all he had. There was no one else to come and support her right now.

Once she'd managed to haphazardly park her car in a space in the car park, she raced to A&E, trying not to think about what she was about to face.

She gave her name and waited and waited, unsure what was taking so long. Was it a bad sign, to be left to wait like this? Or were they just busy?

How she wished there was someone there with her, to provide moral support at least. Her mind went to Jackson, unbidden. They'd spent their whole adult lives together, up until that terrible moment on Blackpool Sands. She'd been to both his grandparents' funerals with him. He'd come and visited her in the hospital when she'd had her appendix out.

If they'd still been together, he would have been the person she'd called. Would he have raced down with her, sat and held her hand, waited in this hell with her? She hoped so. She hoped their relationship hadn't been so awful that he wouldn't have cared.

But it was hard to remember accurately now.

"Miss Thompson?"

Ivy jumped up off the green plastic chair.

"Yes, that's me."

The man before her smiled kindly. "I'm Mr Woods, I'm treating Mr Thompson."

"How is he?" Ivy asked. "Can I see him?"

Mr Woods nodded. "He's asleep right now, and on a lot of pain medication. We believe he has several cracked ribs, and possibly a broken wrist, but our main concern right now is the damage to his head."

Ivy gasped, but the doctor continued.

"He landed on his head. There are cracks to his skull, and we're waiting for a scan to check for brain bleeding."

"Oh my God," Ivy said, swaying slightly. She reached out for the wall to keep her upright. "Will he recover?"

"There's a very good chance he will, Miss Thompson, but I won't lie, it's a major accident, and the older you are, the longer recovery takes."

Ivy nodded, tears filling her eyes. Surely she wasn't going to lose him? This couldn't be happening.

"I'll take you to see him now. Can I ask, are you his next of kin? We may need to operate, and I'll need permission from his next of kin, so if that's someone else..."

"No," Ivy said, wiping away her tears and following him down the corridor. "There's only me."

She was led into a side room, where her dad lay, unconscious, bloody and bruised. Ivy swore under her breath and dug her fingernails into the palm of her hand to stop herself from crying.

"A nurse will be along soon to check his vitals, and then he'll be taken for a CT scan as soon as one becomes available," he said. "And if you have any questions, please just ask."

Ivy nodded, feeling numb, and took a seat in the chair next to the hospital bed. The machines beeped away in the background, and she took Dad's hand, and cried as the doctor left them alone.

"What were you doing on a wall, Dad?" she asked through sobs. "Please be okay. You can't leave me. Please, Dad. I don't know how to live without you."

CHAPTER SEVENTEEN

Ivy fell into an uncomfortable sleep in the chair next to Dad's hospital bed. If she allowed herself to think about it, she might have thought that it was a bit concerning that they were letting her stay the night.

But she couldn't think about it.

She woke up in the middle of the night. The machines were still beeping, and it took her a moment to realise what had woken her.

"We're just taking your dad for another scan," a nurse said, patting her on the arm. "Shouldn't be too long."

Ivy nodded groggily, and watched them wheel him out. He looked so small, lying there asleep. He hadn't woken up since she'd arrived, but the doctors said that was to be expected.

Now she just had to hope the scan didn't show anything terrible. He'd already had a CT earlier that day, but they needed to see how things were progressing, apparently. They'd scared her enough already with talks of brain bleeds and possible surgery. She hoped this scan showed an improvement, and not anything getting worse.

While she waited for him to come back, she pulled

out her phone and checked the time. Three in the morning. Her whole body ached and she longed for her bed. She couldn't believe it was less than twenty-four hours since she had woken up in Alfie's bed, wishing that she could stay there a little longer.

Should she text him to tell him what had happened? Or was that bordering on relationship territory? But she wasn't going to be free to see him tomorrow, or for a while after that most probably... So she was going to have to tell him at some point. And she thought she would feel better once she'd told him.

Feel a little less alone in the world.

Dad's had an accident and I'm in hospital with him. Just wanted you to know. X

She didn't expect an answer, but her phone buzzed in her pocket a few minutes later.

Is he ok? Are you? Anything you need? X

The response made her smile, in spite of everything, and then Dad was wheeled back in, and she quickly typed out a response before putting her phone away.

I don't know yet. I'll let you know X

She wanted to thank him, but she didn't really know what for. Messaging her back in the middle of the night? Asking what he could do? Being there for her, on the end of the phone?

It felt a little pathetic that she was so grateful for a text, and she didn't want to share all of that with him.

"The doctors are just changing shifts," the nurse said in a hushed tone. "But someone will be round to discuss your father's scan sometime this morning."

All Ivy could do was hold Dad's hand, curl up in the chair, and try to get some more sleep. She hoped, once the sun rose, that things would look slightly more positive.

◆ ◆ ◆

When Dad opened his eyes, Ivy cried. The doctor had told her he would wake up, that the bleed on his brain wasn't any bigger, and that they would just monitor it – but it was hard to believe him until she actually saw Dad's eyes open and recognise her.

"Hey," she said with a watery smile.

He reached up a hand to his head, and Ivy grabbed it to stop him. He winced, and she remembered the possible broken wrist.

"Sorry. But you mustn't touch your head. It's really messed up, and you don't want an infection…"

Dad tried to nod, and then winced at that. "Water," he croaked out, and Ivy fumbled to get the cup that had been brought for him, complete with a lid and a straw. She held it up to his mouth and he drank for a moment, before resting his head back on the pillow and closing his eyes.

"What happened, Dad?" Ivy asked. "Andy didn't really know…"

"The guttering was blocked," Dad said croakily, not opening his eyes. "I climbed up the wall on the far side to see what was going on, and must have slipped…"

"You were unconscious when Andy got there," Ivy said. "You shouldn't be climbing up walls, especially with no one around!" she admonished him, feeling guilty that she hadn't been there. Not that she could have stopped him, but at least she would have been there to make sure he didn't lie on the floor unconscious for hours, to call the ambulance, to go with him.

"Yeah yeah," Dad said, sounding exhausted.

"The doctors say you've got a bleed on your brain, but it's not getting bigger. Hopefully you won't need surgery…but this is going to be a long recovery." Ivy reached for his hand, a sob catching in her throat. "I thought I'd lost you, Dad."

He squeezed her hand back, his eyes flickering open. "I'm sorry. I thought that was it, too…"

"Please promise me you'll be more careful. I can't lose you… I don't know how to cope on my own."

"Okay," he said, and it seemed as though even single words exhausted him, but he pushed on. "But you would cope on your own. I'm sure of that."

By the time Dad was moved to a ward, Ivy was struggling to keep her eyes open. She'd not slept in a bed in thirty hours, and the snatches of sleep she'd had in the chair weren't enough to keep her going.

"Go home," Dad said, once the doctor had been round and given them an update. "Get some sleep. Get me some pyjamas – I've had enough of this hospital gown."

He looked very pale, but he was at least talking in full sentences, and that was an improvement. She didn't want to leave him, but she did need to get some clothes for him, and make sure everything was sorted at the farm, at least for now.

"Are you sure?"

"Yes. Go. I'm going to sleep…"

For the next week, Ivy barely slept, barely ate, and barely spent any time at home at all. She travelled back and forth to the hospital, leaving the farmhands, led by Andy, to get whatever they could done at the farm.

Every day Dad seemed stronger, and she was relieved when the risk of the brain bleed getting worse seemed to have subsided. Every night, when visiting hours were over, she went home to the empty farmhouse, and struggled with nightmares about losing Dad, and being alone, and not knowing what to do.

It was the longest week of her life, and never before had she wished for siblings to share the burden so much.

CHAPTER EIGHTEEN

"He's coming home tomorrow," Ivy said, smiling with relief as she chatted to Andy on a quick trip home between hospital visiting hours. "It's going to be a long recovery, but they're happy for him to leave the hospital."

"That's great news," Andy said, gratefully accepting the cup of tea Ivy handed him. "He looked loads better when I went down to see him yesterday."

"Thanks for going. And for keeping things running here – we wouldn't have coped without you."

"Nonsense. Just doing my job."

"You've done more than your job, and you know it," Ivy said.

"I'm just sorry I couldn't get the shop open every day."

"Andy, you must have barely slept, what with being up to milk the cows, getting deliveries out and keeping the farm running," Ivy said, glancing around the kitchen. She would need to give it a good clean before Dad got home. She'd been living off microwave meals and more wine than was sensible of an evening, and not keeping on top of the washing up – and she didn't want him to come home to that.

She didn't know how she was going to manage,

once he was home. The shop needed to be reopened, but someone needed to be with Dad. He wasn't allowed to drive, and he certainly wouldn't be working. So the cows had to be milked, and all the dairy products made, as well as the deliveries done and the shop manned.

She hoped Andy would be willing to do increased hours, along with some of the other lads who worked for them when needed. She could ask Florence, too, who made most of the cheese and butter. But there was still a hell of a lot to manage.

She ran a hand through her long hair, which she hadn't bothered to plait that morning. It would be a knotty, tangled mess by the time bedtime came around.

"Would you mind continuing to milk the cows, for now?" Ivy asked. "We'll obviously pay you for the extra hours, and all the overtime you've done lately. And there's a spare room here, if you want to stay so you don't have to get up so early."

"Of course I can," Andy said.

"And I'll have to figure out the rest somehow..."

When Andy left to get started on jobs that needed doing around the farm, Ivy made herself another cup of tea, and sat down at the kitchen table. She was so relieved that Dad was coming home, and that he was going to be alright – but the panic about their livelihood was well and truly setting in.

The shop being closed during the busiest time of the year was a disaster, really – and with having to pay out extra wages to the staff working harder to make up for both Ivy and her dad Steve being out of action, their finances were going to be seriously affected this month.

Her phone beeped and she grabbed it immediately, just in case it was Dad, or the hospital.

How's it all going? Anything I can do? X

She smiled at the message from Alfie. All week he had sent her messages to check in, and offered to do anything she needed. But she couldn't ask him to do the things she really needed in life, like run the shop or milk the cows. And although she missed seeing him, dragging him into an emotional family situation didn't seem appropriate, either.

But it was nice to know he cared.

Think Dad's coming home tomorrow, she replied quickly.

That's brilliant! The response was quick, and followed by another almost immediately. *I don't want to impose. But if you wanted some company tonight, I could come over? Or you could come here – but I thought you might not want to be away from home. X*

She thought carefully before texting back. Her heart jumped when she first read the words. She'd not seen him in a week, and she missed him.

She gave herself a stern talking-to at that thought. Soon, he would be gone. Missing him wasn't going to help anyone.

And she really needed to focus on Dad.

But… She wasn't allowed to stay at the hospital past seven, anyway. And once Dad was home, she wasn't going to have any time spare at all. Maybe it would be better to spend the evening with Alfie, rather than drinking alone and going to bed early.

She glanced around the kitchen once more. He'd never been out to the farm, and she would definitely need to tidy up – but then she needed to, anyway. And he was right: she felt more comfortable here, where she could rush to Dad at a moment's notice (or ask someone to take her at least, if she'd had a few glasses of wine).

Ivy started to clean up before she texted him back. She told herself she was still deciding, but she knew what she wanted to do.

She just wasn't sure it was sensible.

If you don't mind coming over here, it would be lovely to see you X She texted back eventually, her heart racing.

Of course not. I'm sure I can manage the lanes! I'll bring dinner. What time will you be back from the hospital? X

Warmth flooded through her at the care in the message. It was only a fling, but she couldn't remember being treated so thoughtfully before.

She knew she shouldn't compare.

But it was very hard not to.

After telling him she would be home by eight, she rushed to get the place straightened up, including changing her bed and making sure there were no embarrassing little kid photos on display.

There was so much to sort out. Her mind couldn't even think about how they were going to get through the next few weeks, or months even, with Dad out of action.

Would he ever be able to work on the farm again? It was such a physical job, but she'd never really thought about the fact that a time would come when he wouldn't be able to. Accident or not, he wasn't going to be able to run it forever – and they didn't have a contingency plan.

They only had each other – and she couldn't manage it all alone.

◆ ◆ ◆

When Ivy arrived back home that evening after visiting her dad, she was full of excitement and nerves. It was silly, really – she'd seen Alfie regularly for the past few weeks, and she had not felt nervous every time. But it had been a while this time, and it was the first time he'd visited the farm.

She arrived home a few minutes before eight and was pleased she beat him there. It gave her a minute to run in and check her appearance in the mirror before his sports car pulled in behind hers on the drive.

She couldn't wipe the smile off her face when opening the door. She had missed him. Whether or not that was sensible was a whole other matter, but it was true. She couldn't help it.

"Hey," he said, leaning in to kiss her lightly on the lips. It sent delicious shivers running through her body.

"Hey." She stood back to let him enter and closed the door behind him. "You found the place okay?"

"I set off a bit earlier than I needed to, in case I got lost – which I did," he said with a laugh. "But I'm getting pretty used to driving on the lanes around here."

"You'll get a shock when you're driving on big roads in the city again," Ivy said, trying not to let sadness tinge her words. She didn't want to look pathetic. And it wasn't fair to guilt trip him over leaving, when that was always what he was going to do.

"How's your dad?" he asked, unpacking a delicious-smelling Chinese takeaway onto the kitchen table. "This place looks amazing, by the way. I'd love to see it in the proper daylight."

Ivy wondered if he was just being polite. The little farm wasn't much – but then, she supposed she was just used to it. It had been her home ever since she was born.

"He's looking forward to coming home, I think, although a bit nervous about how he's going to manage the stairs. And he keeps going on about the work on the farm, which he's obviously not going to be able to do. His arm is going to be in a cast for a few weeks still."

"Have you got a plan for that? I'm happy to help in any way I can, although I'm afraid milking cows is probably outside of my skill set."

Ivy laughed, finding it hard to picture the beautiful Alfie, with his perfect mop of blond hair, sitting on a milking stool beneath one of the cows. Not that they milked by hand very often any more – but still, she didn't think he'd be confident herding cows into the barn, or using the milking machine. "Thank you," she said, grabbing the bottle of wine from the fridge. "I'll figure it out. Somehow."

"As long as it doesn't involve you working even more hours," Alfie said, glancing around and then grabbing two wine glasses from the sideboard. "You work crazy hours as it is."

"Not all of us can afford to take the summer off, though," she said, pouring the wine. She winced as the words replayed in her mind, and when she glanced up, there was definitely hurt in Alfie's sparkling blue eyes.

"I'm sorry. I shouldn't have said that. We just live completely different lives. I know how hard you work. I'm just exhausted..." she babbled, worried that she'd hurt him, worried that she'd ruined their evening.

"It's okay," Alfie said with a shrug. "If that's the way you feel, I get it. I know I'm privileged. Although I do work very hard most of the time...but I guess you'll just have to take my word for it."

Ivy put down the wine and grabbed his hands. "No, Alfie, I don't think that. It was a stupid thing for me to say. I'm sorry. Can we forget it? Please?"

She was embarrassed to find that her eyes were

filling with tears. It was all too much. She hadn't meant to snap at him. He'd brought her dinner, come over to spend the evening with her, even after she'd ignored him for most of the week.

"Hey, hey," Alfie said, pulling one hand away from hers and cupping her cheek with it. "It's okay. I was being sensitive. Just ignore me. And I really do want to help, if there's anything you think I can do."

"Thank you," she said in a half whisper, leaning into his soft touch. "It's just all been so much. This whole summer... I already felt alone. And now, it just makes it even more apparent that I only have Dad. And he only has me. And it's just too much, to rely so heavily on another person. To wonder what if..." A sob escaped her mouth, choking off her words, and she closed her eyes and tried to push away the tears.

She didn't want to do this. She didn't want to cry in front of Alfie. Things between them were meant to be fun and light-hearted, with no strings attached. He didn't want to come here and comfort a crying woman.

But he pulled her in close, held her to his solid chest, and stroked her hair while she sobbed.

She didn't know how much time had passed when she finally pulled her head away and blinked up at him with red eyes. "I'm sorry, Alfie. Maybe I should have said no tonight. I'm a mess. But I wanted to see you..."

He tipped her chin up with one finger and pressed his lips to hers for a moment. "I wanted to see you too," he said, and the words sounded so genuine that they made Ivy weak at the knees. "Let's eat this takeaway, before it goes cold," he said. "I hope I picked something you'll like, I went for a few options to be safe. And then, if you just want to be alone, I'll go – no offence taken."

Ivy was confident she wasn't going to want him to go, but she didn't trust herself to speak again without crying, so she simply nodded and took a seat at the table beside him.

He really had brought a wide selection: quite possibly something from every section of the menu. She loaded her plate up, realising she hadn't eaten all day, and took a large swig of her wine.

"Thanks for this," she said. "So, what have you been up to, while I've been in the hospital?"

They ate and chatted until it was pitch black outside, and Alfie told her about the final contenders for his parents' new holiday home, and how he'd swum in the sea at Torcross, and how busy the campsite was.

"I hate that you feel so alone," Alfie said when there was a lull in the conversation.

Ivy felt her cheeks turning bright red. She hadn't meant to admit that.

"I know I haven't known you long. I know I'm leaving, I know me saying this doesn't help anything at all, but I just need you to know that I don't like thinking of you being lonely. You don't deserve to be alone."

Ivy smiled weakly. "If only you didn't live so far away," she said.

Alfie reached across and took her hand. "If only."

Her heart raced at the contact. His words didn't change anything, they couldn't, but they made her feel like someone cared.

And that did help.

"I know you were in a serious relationship, before I met you," Alfie said and Ivy cringed, wondering how much Christi, Oscar, and Olivia had told him. She herself had barely mentioned Jackson to him. Never by name, certainly. "And I hope that this…*thing* between us hasn't hurt you. Because I never intended…"

Ivy reached up to place a finger to his lips to silence him. He blinked, but did not say any more.

"You've got nothing to apologise for, Alfie," she said. "And neither have I. My life hasn't gone the way I thought it would, it's true. And my dad getting hurt… It's made me realise how fragile things are."

She took her finger away from his lips. "But this has been a wonderful summer, I promise you. And if I'm lonely once you've gone back to your real life, then that's not your fault."

"I'll miss you," Alfie said, and she nearly started crying again. "I probably shouldn't say that. I know this was just a summer fling. But I will."

"I'll miss you too." She wasn't sure if admitting it out loud was a good idea, but it was the truth and it spilt from her lips effortlessly.

He pulled her in for a kiss that sent a shiver down her spine, and the food was forgotten, and the wine was forgotten, and all of Ivy's worries and fears and tears were put on hold, as she led him up to her bedroom.

The teenage purple walls didn't seem such a big deal any more.

CHAPTER NINETEEN

With Dad home, Ivy was saved the time she had been spending driving backwards and forwards to the hospital, but it was filled with so many other jobs. Dad was doing much better, but he couldn't manage the stairs on his own, he couldn't stand for very long without getting dizzy, and he needed help getting his medication every couple of hours.

She certainly couldn't leave him, at least not for more than an hour or so, but the shop needed to be opened the following day, or they were going to be in financial trouble.

"It's so good to have you home, Dad," Ivy said, sitting down to eat lunch with him. He was still battered and bruised, but the blood had all been washed off, and he was looking a much healthier colour.

"It's good to be home," he said with a smile. "Although I hate that I'm leaving all the work to you. You look exhausted…"

Ivy waved away his concerns with one hand. "I've got it under control, Dad, don't worry."

But when he went to bed for a nap that afternoon, she worried that she very definitely did not have it under control.

Even if she could find enough staff to fill the gaps of all the things that she and Dad normally got done in a day, how would she afford to pay them?

A knock on the door disturbed her panic. When she went to answer it, she found Christi standing on the doorstep.

"Hey." She embraced her friend and stood back to let her in. "You didn't have to come out here," she said, closing the door behind her. "I know how much you've got on. I really appreciate you texting to check in; I know you're busy."

"What are friends for?" she said, putting a big bag down on the kitchen table. "I brought you some supplies, thought you might not have had a chance to get to the shops. Now, how's your dad?"

Ivy wondered if Alfie had said something to Christi to make her feel she needed to come out here. Maybe her unexpected crying fit had made him concerned.

"He's doing better. Sleeping now."

"Good. That means we can put the kettle on and have a little chat."

Ivy made the tea, wondering why specifically Christi was there, and then joined her at the kitchen table. She had a notebook in front of her, but Ivy couldn't read what was written on it upside down.

"Right," Christi said in that organised way of hers. "I've made a rota, but I don't know the ins and outs of dairy life, so you'll have to tell me if I've missed anything."

Ivy frowned. "I don't know what you mean."

"You can't run this place, the shop, the deliveries, and take care of your dad all by yourself."

"Well, no. But I don't know—"

"So that's what the rota is for. I spoke to Andy when

he brought the delivery. He said he's agreed to carry on milking the cows and keep on top of any farm work, with a couple of the other farmhands. And the lady that makes the cheese and the butter will up her hours, so there's no slack for you to pick up there, like you normally do."

"Oh." Ivy's eyes widened. It was so kind of Christi to organise things, but Ivy didn't know where she was going to find the money to pay these people for the extra hours.

"Now the shop was easy to sort; Aunt Olivia has several elderly friends who are quite happy to sit in there and run it, and have a chat with anyone who walks through the door. The deliveries I've got Oscar overseeing. He won't do all of them, but he's got some friends who are happy to drive and know the area well."

Ivy blanched. "Christi, this is so nice of you. And everyone. But I don't think I can afford—"

"No one wants paying, Ivy. Well, your regular staff I'm sure will expect their normal wages. But everyone else – they're volunteering. For the rest of the summer, at least. No one wants you to lose the best revenue of the year."

Ivy's eyes filled with tears. It was becoming a bit of a habit.

"I can't ask them to—"

"You didn't ask them to. I did. And no one is doing it unwillingly, I promise you. You might want to give them a basket of cheese at the end of the summer, but they're not expecting any money. Everyone knows how hard you work, how hard your dad works, and that you couldn't have predicted this."

Ivy sipped her too-hot tea just to have something to do to stop herself from crying.

Christi reached across the table and took Ivy's

hand. "When I'd made a pig's ear of the campsite, you all came and helped. It's what we do around here, isn't it?"

Ivy nodded. "I guess. But this is a lot..."

"And we've got a plan. You'll look after your dad, and everything else will be taken care of. And if I've missed anything important, just let me know, I'm sure I can find someone else to rope in. Alfie did offer to be part of the rota, but I wasn't sure I could see him milking cows," Christi said with a wink.

Ivy laughed. "I said the same to him. But it's sweet that he wants to help."

"It is sweet. He seems like a really nice guy. It's a shame he doesn't live round here."

"It is," Ivy said with a sniff. "But that's just the way life goes, isn't it? You know, I felt so alone, and this has reminded me of why I love living here. Of how amazing it is to know that there are people you can rely on, even when they're not family."

◆ ◆ ◆

"Do you mind if I nip out and meet a friend for coffee?" Ivy asked her dad a week later. He was so much more stable now, but she didn't like to leave him. "I'll only be an hour, and I'll have my phone on me."

"Go, go, you've been cooped up here far too much. Andy's on the farm if I really need someone – which I won't," he added when she looked concerned.

"If you're sure..." She didn't really want to leave him, but she was feeling a bit stir-crazy. And having seen Alfie so regularly at the beginning of the summer, she was very aware of the fact that the summer was coming to an end, and she didn't have much longer to see him.

So when he'd texted and asked her to join him for

coffee, she couldn't bear to say no.

He'd suggested a little café overlooking Torcross beach, and she appreciated the fact that he'd chosen somewhere pretty close to home for her. It also reminded her that she hadn't set foot on a beach in almost three months since Jackson had left.

And it was surely time to remedy that.

How had it been nearly three months? In some ways, it felt like a lifetime. And in others, like it still wasn't real. In the spring, she'd had no idea that her life would look so very different by the autumn.

Alfie was already waiting, looking drop-dead gorgeous in a polo shirt, chino shorts, and sunglasses. His skin was tanned from the beautiful summer they had been having and his hair was even more blond than when he'd arrived.

He greeted her with a kiss, as he always did, and took hold of her hand, not letting go even when they sat down and ordered coffees.

The sound of the sea hitting the shingle made Ivy ache to swim in it, or at least dip her toes.

"How are you doing?"

Ivy considered the answer before replying. "Not going to break down in tears, if that's a good answer?"

Alfie grinned. "Definitely. Things are looking up?"

"Yeah. Everyone pitching in is amazing. I think we'll make it through the summer, and then I'll figure out what Dad can do. And what I want to do."

"You don't want to keep doing what you've been doing?" Alfie asked, thanking the waitress who brought out their coffees.

"I don't know. I love it here. And I love what I do. But I don't want to blink and be thirty and not know what I've done with my life. Anyway, you said you had news in your message?"

"Oh, yeah. I had an offer accepted – well, an offer with my parents' money."

"You've bought their holiday home?" Ivy's heart dropped. The end of August was fast approaching, and she'd known they would have to say goodbye soon, but would this rob them of their final ten days?

"Yeah. They signed off on it. They've not even seen it in person, so I hope they like it! I went with the one in Hope Cove. I think it's got everything they'll want. And if I want to come down for a holiday…"

"You won't have to pay over the odds for Christi's yurt," Ivy said with a smile. She hadn't let herself think that he might come back again, for holidays.

Maybe she would see him again.

Although she would, she hoped, settle down in a long-term relationship again in the not-too-distant future. She still wanted marriage, and a family, even if things with Jackson hadn't panned out.

But seeing Alfie again, in a different context, wouldn't be easy.

It turned out a fling wasn't as simple as she'd imagined.

That was a thought for another day, though.

"I'm so happy you found somewhere," she said. "And got the paperwork done before you have to leave!"

"I know, I didn't think it was going to get sorted. It'll be a while before they exchange and get the keys, but that'll be down to Mum and Dad."

Alfie told her about the house as they finished their coffees, and showed her photos of the beautiful view. Ivy couldn't imagine being able to afford a place like that at all, let alone as a second home.

It was as she'd told Alfie: they came from different worlds.

"Do you have to get straight back?" Alfie asked.

Ivy glanced at her phone, both to check the time and to see if Dad had tried to get hold of her. "I've got a little bit longer."

"Fancy a walk on the beach?"

She hesitated for a moment. She'd avoided her favourite places in the world all summer. And she really wanted to stroll along with Alfie, and enjoy the sun, and feel the sea on her feet.

But what if...

"Yes," she said, ignoring her worries. They were stupid. Nothing bad was going to happen. Jackson would have broken up with her wherever she had suggested they meet – she could see that now.

As Alfie took Ivy's hand and they walked down the concrete steps onto the shingle beach, Ivy felt like she was coming home.

She'd been a fool to stay away from the beach for so long. This was what she loved. One of the reasons she never wanted to leave this place. Yes, she'd had her heart broken on Blackpool Sands – but that wasn't the fault of that beach, let alone all the other beautiful beaches in the area.

"One second," Ivy said, pausing to bend down and take off her sandals. "Can we walk down to the sea? I love walking along where the water hits the sand. Or the pebbles, I suppose I should say here."

"Of course. I didn't realise you loved the beach so much." It highlighted to Ivy how little he really knew her...and how much Jackson had ruined.

"It's my favourite place. But..." The pebbles were sharp beneath her feet, and she winced as one caught the arch of her foot in the wrong place. "We had a bit of a falling out," she said with a laugh, not really sure she wanted to tell Alfie any more.

"I'm glad you're friends again," he said with a smile, not pushing, not laughing at her ridiculous statement.

Her heart felt like it might explode. He was such a good man. Handsome, funny, caring... Why couldn't he live here? Why had she met him at a time in her life when everything was up in the air and she had no idea where she was heading?

Her feet hit the cold ocean, and she gasped and laughed. There was no point in thinking that way. Maybe things were so perfect because nothing was leading anywhere. She didn't know much about him, aside from the fact that he was rich, and all of the positive traits she had witnessed. She didn't know whether he'd had serious relationships, whether he had flings everywhere he went, whether he'd been married, had children. She presumed at some point over the last few weeks he would have mentioned it if he was divorced or a distant father of unnamed children.

But maybe he wouldn't have done. They were living in the moment, and Ivy had to remind herself to remain there. Not to think about the past. Not to worry about the future. But just to enjoy the moment they were living in. Alfie unlaced his trainers and dipped his own feet into the sea.

"It's always cold," he said with a laugh. "Does it ever warm up?"

Ivy laughed. "Not really. But you get used to it."

"I'd be tempted to have a dip if I'd brought my

trunks. I'd go in my boxers, but—" he gestured to the crowded beach. "Probably not appropriate."

Ivy couldn't control her giggles. "Probably not. Next time, eh?" Both were very aware that there weren't many next times left, but neither mentioned it now.

Alfie took her hands in his, and as the cold sea lapped at their feet, he leaned down and pressed a spine-tingling kiss to her lips. It wasn't a proposal on a beach, that was for sure, but she thought it was the most romantic thing she'd ever experienced on one of her beloved beaches.

"I've never had a summer as wonderful as this one," Alfie said, his blue eyes sparkling in the sunshine. "I just want you to know that."

Ivy licked her lips, which had suddenly gone very dry. She wanted to say the same back, but she couldn't quite figure out if it was true. The summer with Alfie had been wonderful. Dad's accident had been terrible. And everything before the summer... Well, she would never be the same again, that was for sure.

She'd never known such highs and lows before, but that didn't seem the right thing to say in the face of Alfie's romantic declaration.

"I'm so glad you came here for the summer," she said in the end. "And I'm so glad I met you."

And then they kissed again, not caring who was watching, not worrying about how cold their feet were in the sea. They kissed as though it was their very last chance to do so.

And it wouldn't be too long, Ivy reflected sadly when she got home that evening, until that was the case.

CHAPTER TWENTY

The final week before Alfie's planned departure was the quickest week Ivy had ever known. She was so busy looking after Dad, and making sure every facet of the business was running smoothly, with the amazing volunteers Christi had pulled together, that she barely had time to eat, let alone sleep – and what she really wanted to do was spend time with Alfie.

"Andy's spending the night in the spare room tonight," Dad said over breakfast one morning. "He's got so much to do, and he needs to start even earlier than usual."

"I'm glad he's staying, but I feel terrible that there's so much for him to do…"

"I'm hoping I'll be back out there by next month," Dad said.

"Don't push yourself, though. You know what the doctor said…"

"Yeah, I'm old, take it easy, yada yada," Dad said with a roll of his eyes. "Anyway. That's not why I said it. Why don't you go out for the night? See Christi, if you like. Stay out. I'm fine now, and if I need anything, Andy will be here.

Ivy hesitated. It was a perfect suggestion, really. She'd only seen Alfie for an hour here or there since Dad's accident. The thought of a whole night…

But what if something happened? What if Dad needed her? What if…

"Stop worrying, I can see it in your eyes. Go on, have a night off from babysitting me. I'll be fine."

"It's not babysitting, Dad," Ivy said with a fond smile. She texted Alfie as soon as he went up for a shower.

It felt odd going to the campsite to see him, when she hadn't in a while. And knowing that it would very likely be the last night they spent together was affecting her more than she wanted to admit.

When she got to the yurt he'd been calling home for the last couple of months, butterflies fluttered in her stomach.

She felt too much for this man.

She was going to break her own heart.

And yet here she was, coming back for more.

The table had a candle in the middle, and a bunch of wildflowers, and Alfie had a sheepish grin on his face.

"I wanted to cook for you," he said. "It's only pasta, though. I'm not a great cook anyway, and there's not much I can manage with just a hob…"

"That's really sweet," Ivy said, a smile taking over her face. "I can't remember the last time someone cooked for me."

He poured her a glass of wine, and it felt just like a real date.

Which she knew was silly, because he was leaving soon, and she might never see him again.

Maybe this had all been a mistake.

If she could go back in time, and wallow in misery for the whole summer after Jackson left her, instead of throwing herself into this fling with Alfie, would she have done so?

He put down a bowl of pasta in front of her, and her heart flipped at the smile he gave her.

No, she didn't think she would change this summer. Even if it was going to lead to misery.

"I'm so glad you could come over," he said, taking a seat opposite her. "Is your dad doing okay?"

She nodded. "Much better. He wants to get back out to work as soon as he can, but I don't think he should push himself…"

"It's good that he's thinking about it though, right? He must be starting to feel better."

They ate in silence for a few moments, and Ivy realised just how hungry she was. It was surprising, since she wasn't doing all the physical work that she normally did, yet she was hungrier than ever. Stress-eating, she supposed.

"So, you know I'm leaving on Sunday…" Alfie said, breaking the silence.

Ivy swallowed the pasta and took a moment to get control over her emotions.

"Yeah."

"I feel like…like maybe we should have discussed things a bit more. Before all of this started."

Was he having regrets? Ivy ate a mouthful of pasta to have a reason not to speak for a moment. What was the point in telling her now, if he did? He was leaving in four days.

"I know everything happened pretty quickly, and then kept happening, and we didn't really discuss expectations, or anything, other than that I was leaving…"

"I'm not expecting anything from you," Ivy said a little harshly.

"No, I didn't mean..." Alfie ran a hand through his blond hair, his cheeks flushing a little pink. "I'm saying this all wrong. I just want you to know... I don't do this sort of thing. Normally."

Ivy raised her eyebrows. "Oh?" What was this handsome man before her trying to say?

"I'm not a monk, or anything, but I don't have endless strings of short-term flings."

A smile crept onto Ivy's face. "I don't, either," she said. *I've literally only slept with one other man but you,* she thought to herself, but that wasn't something she needed to share with him. He'd surely read into it, think she was putting far more importance on this...fling than she ought to be.

And whilst that was possibly true, he didn't need to know it.

"I know we come from very different worlds. And I have to leave, and I live a couple of hundred miles away, and this has to come to an end. But I guess what I want you to know is...this was special. To me. And I won't forget it."

Sadness filled her heart, but she smiled anyway. His words meant a lot, even though they didn't change anything. This was real life, not some fairytale. It had been a magical summer, and now it would have to come to an end.

"It's been special to me, too," Ivy said, reaching out across the table to take Alfie's hand. He gave her one of those heart-stopping smiles, and she had to tell herself not to let her emotions overwhelm her. To live in the moment, to enjoy this night.

She could wallow once he was gone.

CHAPTER TWENTY-ONE

"Are you okay?" Dad asked over breakfast on Sunday morning. Although she had made them both scrambled eggs, she couldn't face eating any. Her stomach felt queasy, and every time she thought of Alfie leaving later that day, she wanted to cry.

"Yeah," she said, trying to think of a lie so she wouldn't have to tell Dad why she wasn't herself. "Think I'm coming down with something."

"It's been a stressful few weeks," he said, tucking into his breakfast. "And I know you've taken on a lot of it by yourself. You should take a holiday, once I'm well enough to work again."

"Yeah, maybe," Ivy said, pushing the food around her plate with her fork. There was no way they were going to have the time or the money for her to take a holiday. The volunteers had been incredible, but she couldn't expect them to keep helping past the end of the season. And even then, they'd had to drop some of the extra tasks around the farm. Once Dad was working again, it was going to take both of them working hard to get back to where they had been before the accident.

At least he was okay to be left for short periods now. Soon, she would be able to get back to running the shop herself. Maybe open extra days, to make up for the lost revenue. Although the busiest season of the year would be over...

Still, she'd have plenty of free time to throw into the business.

"I'm going to nip out to the supermarket later, if that's okay?" she said.

"Course. We're nearly out of coffee..."

"Already on my list," Ivy said.

A trip to the supermarket seemed like a decent enough excuse to leave and say goodbye to Alfie. Dad had no idea about him, which was how she wanted to keep it, but she couldn't let him go without saying goodbye.

She wanted to cry the whole drive over to Salcombe. Knowing that he was going to leave didn't seem to lessen the pain.

Was it the same pain as when Jackson left? She wasn't sure, because she hadn't seen that coming. The pain of that was magnified by feeling that so many years had been wasted, and that her future wouldn't look how she had imagined it.

Whereas this fling had simply postponed her future. She had always known it wouldn't change it.

He was waiting outside when she got there. He looked uncomfortable, standing by his car under the cloudy sky. Ivy could see Christi, Oscar, and Olivia glancing out of the cottage window, clearly expecting her arrival.

She was thankful they were giving them some space.

"Hey," she said as she stepped out of the car. "You ready to go?" She could see the car was packed up, but she needed to make some sort of conversation, else she would just stand and weep.

"Yeah," he said, running a hand through his hair. "Thought I'd better head off before the rain they're predicting starts."

"Sorry I couldn't get here sooner."

"It's okay."

The conversation was so stilted, but Ivy didn't know how to make it easier. Neither of them was happy to say goodbye, that much was obvious, but there was no way to change the facts.

"I should let you go," Ivy said, the awkward atmosphere making her cringe.

He nodded. "Don't be a stranger, hey?"

"You too," she said, because what else could she say? But she wasn't sure how texting each other every now and again was going to make this easier. When what she really wanted was to date him. It was something she could admit to herself, now that he was leaving. It wasn't possible, but it was what she wanted, and so staying in touch would surely just be more painful.

But tempting, nonetheless.

"Bye, then."

He reached out, and she thought he was going to shake her hand, and her heart ached at how cold things were – but then he pulled her in towards him, and lowered his lips to hers, and kissed her so thoroughly that she thought her knees might give way.

"Goodbye, Alfie," she whispered when he pulled away.

He rested his forehead against hers for a moment. "Thank you, for a wonderful summer," he said, and then he let go of her hand, and got in his car.

And Ivy's heart broke.

She watched him drive away, waving and smiling and fighting back the tears that were so desperate to fall.

When he disappeared out of sight, a sob ripped through her body, and she turned away from the cottage so no one would see her misery.

It was a different pain to the one when Jackson had left. That had been a shock, and it had run deep, and it had thrown her off course.

This was sharp, and expected, and devastating because it had disrupted such a happy time.

"Ivy?" The soft voice behind her made her jump, and when she turned, Christi was standing there, looking concerned. "Are you okay?"

Ivy's first instinct was to lie. But the words wouldn't come. So she shook her head, and allowed Christi to pull her into a tight hug as she cried.

"I told him not to break your heart," Christi said with a sigh.

It's not his fault, Ivy thought, her tears stopping words from coming. *I knew what I was doing. Or I thought I did. I've broken my own heart.*

◆ ◆ ◆

She couldn't go to the supermarket in that state, and although Christi offered her a cup of tea, she didn't really want to be around anyone. She had to get herself under control before she could go home. She couldn't turn up in tears, else she'd have to explain what had happened to Dad, and that wasn't something she wanted to do.

She drove without thinking, and she was surprised when she found herself in the car park of Blackpool Sands beach.

She hadn't been there since that fateful day in May, and she wasn't sure why she'd brought herself here, to a place where she had experienced such pain.

But it was still a place that she loved, and so she gingerly got out of the car, and wandered over to the grass overlooking the beach.

It was very quiet. With the summer season over, and clouds filling the sky, the only people on the beach were dog walkers and parents trying to get their kids to waste some excess energy.

She couldn't bring herself to step onto the golden sands, and so instead sat cross-legged on the grass and looked out over the place that she loved so much.

And she let all of the tears out. All of the pain and hurt and frustration that she had been bottling up.

She'd thought Jackson had torn out her heart on this beach. That she would never feel the same again.

And then she'd stumbled across Alfie – and maybe she didn't feel the same, but she definitely felt *something*.

Maybe it was just lust. It felt like more, but perhaps that was because it had been a rebound fling, or because it had been short-lived, or because things with Jackson had been stale for so long beforehand.

She could admit it now. There was no point in lying to herself.

If Alfie lived here, maybe it wouldn't have worked out. Could you jump from an eight-year relationship with someone you thought you were going to marry, straight into something else?

Maybe it would have hurt less if she'd had the choice.

Her misery over Jackson no longer filled her days, but if it was just going to be replaced with misery over Alfie, and how she had no idea where her life was heading, she wasn't sure she was in a much better position than she had been back in May.

Rain began to fall, but Ivy couldn't face going home just yet. She got up, took a deep breath, and stepped out onto the sand. It crunched beneath her trainers and she took slow, measured steps towards the sea, while everyone else made their way back to their cars.

What was she going to do with her life? Alfie, and the summer, had only been a way to put off thinking about it.

Now she had to return to reality, and she needed a plan. She didn't want to let misery overwhelm her.

As she walked, she let her mind wander. Maybe she ought to leave Devon. She'd always wanted to stay, but maybe she'd been wrong. Maybe happiness was waiting for her somewhere else.

But then she thought about everything she would be leaving – her beloved beaches, the business, and most importantly, her dad – and she rejected that idea. There was nowhere else she wanted to go. If she moved, she'd just be miserable and broke and alone somewhere else.

Even more alone.

At least here she had her family, the community, and some good friends.

She couldn't date for a while, she decided as the rain just got heavier. It had been such a hot, dry summer – but when it rained, it certainly poured. Her heart was too broken for another relationship to be a good idea. And this fling with Alfie, and the way she felt now, seemed to prove to her that she was no good at casual.

So she didn't want to move, and she didn't want to date.

But she did need a plan.

She wanted to move out. To start her life properly, as an adult. Maybe to expand the business. Christi seemed so happy, running the campsite, expanding it, and now doing up the mansion in Malborough, adding another string to her bow.

Maybe if Ivy threw herself into the dairy, and made it bigger and better, she could be as happy. Would Christi be as happy running her businesses if she didn't have Oscar to go home to at night? Ivy pushed away the thought. It was no good thinking about it. Her 'Oscar' – whether that was Jackson or Alfie – was gone.

As she made her way back to her car, soaked through and still not sure whether she was still crying or if it was just the rain, she knew she needed to make a plan, so that she wasn't still feeling like this in a year's time.

She paid for her parking and then remembered that she still needed to go to the supermarket. She had no idea how long she'd been gone for, but she hoped Dad wasn't worrying.

She had to get back to her real life – and learn to be happy in it again.

CHAPTER TWENTY-TWO

When Dad told her he wanted to go out on the farm with Andy for a bit, she wondered if she ought to dissuade him – but he looked so excited to be out and about, and she wasn't really in the mood to chat. She'd managed to pass off her red eyes and tired face as the start of a cold, but she didn't want Dad asking questions about why she was so miserable again.

She watched him heading out with Andy in the tractor, feeling slightly nervous, and then returned to the kitchen. She had surprisingly little to do, without Dad there to run around after. There were so many bits of the business that needed running, but she couldn't do that from her kitchen table.

What she could do, though, she thought as she sat down with a cup of tea, was think about what she wanted to do with her life. Because she'd decided she wanted to stay in Devon, and that she didn't want a new relationship right now.

But she did want a plan.

What could she do, though? They already had deliveries and the shop, both of which she had started. But If she was going to move out, they needed to up their revenue – and she wanted something more. Something she could really sink her teeth into. Something that could be entirely hers.

The house suddenly felt too small, and she grabbed her car keys, needing to get out for a bit. She couldn't think straight, and when she stood up, a wave of dizziness caught her by surprise.

She really needed to get some more sleep.

She sat in the driver's seat of the car for a few minutes, making sure she wasn't dizzy any more, and trying to decide where to go. She wanted to get out, but she couldn't be long. Dad would wonder where she was, if he got back and found the house empty. And she still didn't like leaving him for long.

In the end, she drove down Slapton line, blasted music and opened the windows, even though it was starting to drizzle. And then she pulled into the car park, turned around, and drove it again.

The little café by the beach was busy, in spite of the rain brewing, as was the pub, but the beach was pretty empty.

Ivy parked up opposite the row of businesses and watched people going about their lives as the rain began to pour. A couple clutched takeaway cups of coffee and dashed to their car. A dog walker ran to the little butcher's in the town square. A mother put down her umbrella at the door of the café and struggled to push her pram in.

And then an idea came to Ivy. She didn't know if it had any legs. She didn't know if it would be possible. But the image of her own little café, stocking the produce of the dairy, but its own entity, filled her mind. On the seafront, maybe. Perhaps not this seafront…but one of them. There were many beaches, after all, and not all of them had cafés nearby.

Her own business, and working overlooking the sea.

It seemed perfect.

Realising the time, she started her engine and hurried back home, hoping Dad hadn't got soaked in the rain, or slipped over, or forgotten to take his tablets.

But the idea of the café didn't leave her mind, and she resolved to look into it properly, as soon as she had some free time.

◆ ◆ ◆

When the dizzy feeling returned later that week, she blamed it on the long list of figures in front of her at the kitchen table. She didn't think writing a business plan came naturally to her, but she had no one, aside from the internet, to ask for advice.

Her five-year plan was centred around her starting up her own café, stocked with the dairy's produce. Ideally, she would find a premises with a flat above it – and that would tick off another of her goals.

But if she was going to do that, she needed capital, and so a business plan to present to the bank was necessary.

She'd done her research. She knew what her outgoings would be, and she had some rough projections for takings. She knew, too, that she could get the produce from the dairy at a very reduced rate. And she could bake herself, and work every hour under the sun…

But staring at the numbers was making her feel queasy, and she pushed them to one side with a sigh.

Dad would be happy to help, but he didn't really have a head for numbers, either. And besides, she really wanted to do this on her own. Her project, her arm of the business. Her plan for the rest of her life.

She knew she wanted to stay in Devon – but now she knew what she wanted to do, too. And the thought was exciting, and terrifying, all at the same time. Because having something she really wanted meant she had something to lose.

She looked out of the kitchen window, where the grass was waving lazily in the breeze, and allowed herself to very briefly think of Alfie. They'd shared a couple of texts, but there was no reason for any real contact, and she'd known that would be the case from day one.

It had been a beautiful, exciting summer fling. Exactly what she had needed to get through the pain of her break-up with Jackson.

And now she just needed to figure out who she was alone. And how she was going to move forwards.

A wave of nausea hit her, and she ran to the bathroom, only just making it in time to throw up. Sitting on the cold bathroom floor, in case the sickness struck again, she tried to think what she had eaten that could have made her sick.

Her stomach rumbled, and she pulled herself up, wondering if it was just stress.

It was only as she was making herself some toast that the question came into her mind.

She'd been on the pill since she was a teenager. And her period had never been a day late. She knew lots of people had issues with hormonal contraception, but she'd not been one of them. It had always worked like clockwork for her.

Except now she was dizzy. And sick. And she couldn't think when she'd last had her period.

Panic spiralled through her mind as she sat down

with her toast, suddenly ravenous, and checked her phone – but for some reason, she'd not recorded her dates for a couple of months.

Because she'd been having too much fun?

Or because she hadn't had anything to record?

A whole summer of uninterrupted fun...

Her hand was shaking as she lifted the toast to her mouth. She couldn't be, could she? She and Alfie had been careful. She was sure they had been. Even when they'd been drunk...

But the more she thought about it, the more it all started to add up. The tiredness. The dizziness. The emotions she couldn't control.

And now, the sickness.

She grabbed her keys from the side, knowing she had to find out. She couldn't sit and obsess all day, nor go to work the following day without knowing. And there was no way she could go to the local pharmacy. She knew both the women who worked there, and would undoubtedly run into a customer she knew as well. And then the whole area would know that she at least suspected she might be pregnant.

No, she would have to drive further away, to a supermarket. Somewhere she could buy it without anyone commenting. Because if it was true, she didn't want anyone to know. And if it wasn't – well, she didn't want to be the topic of conjecture.

After furtively paying for the cheapest test she could find in the supermarket, she had to decide where to take it. The toilets of the supermarket seemed too stressful, but she didn't want to have to go home and find Dad waiting for her, stopping her from being able to take it with chat. Or worse still, if he saw the test in her hand, or in the rubbish afterwards. He was working more and more now, but he was still often in the house in the middle of the day.

Although she dithered by the automatic doors of the supermarket for a few moments, in the end she got back in her car and drove home. The clouds above her looked white, and she only hoped that the rain forecast for the day would hold off, and Dad would stay out on the farm for more of the afternoon. After such a beautiful, hot summer, the autumn was turning out to be grey and wet.

Her heart racing, she parked up and snuck in through the back door, hoping she could avoid Dad even if he'd come in for lunch. But a quick peak told her the kitchen was mercifully empty, and so she ran upstairs to her ensuite, wanting to take the test as soon as possible.

Her hands shook as she opened it, read the instructions, then panicked and reread them.

And then she just had to wait.

Five minutes ticked by painfully slowly.

I can't be pregnant.

We were careful.

What a disaster it would be if I was.

I'm all alone…

A wave of nausea washed over her, and she could only hope it was from the stress.

When the alarm on her phone sounded that the time was up, she took a deep breath, and turned to look at the little stick that had the power to change her life.

And there was no doubting the result. Even to a pregnancy-test-taking novice like her. Even when she'd bought the cheapest one available.

Two very strong, very dark lines.

Pregnant.

◆ ◆ ◆

None of it seemed real.

She sat on her bedroom floor, holding that stick, staring at it and not believing it, for a very long time. The sky outside grew dusky, and Dad called up to her. She shouted down an excuse about feeling ill, and told him there were leftovers in the fridge, and that she would be down soon.

But it was so hard to drag herself up from the bedroom floor.

How had she ended up here?

Pregnant, single, living at home. She didn't even know how far gone she was. She was sure she'd had a period after Jackson...so at least the identity of the father wasn't in question.

Father.

Her summer fling had certainly left her with long-reaching consequences...and Alfie too.

If she told him.

She couldn't imagine doing that.

And she had options. She didn't have to tell him. She didn't have to carry on with this pregnancy.

Dinner with Dad that evening was a very quiet affair. He tried to start a conversation a few times, but Ivy just didn't have the room in her brain to think of anything else.

She picked at her spaghetti, her stomach churning, and let her mind race. There was no use trying to control it. There was just too much going on.

Should she text Alfie? She had his number, after all. They'd said they wouldn't be strangers...

But he was in Oxford, living his life. He'd probably forgotten all about her already. What the hell would she even text? *Just found out I'm pregnant, think it's yours, might not keep it?*

And if she did decide to keep it... She didn't want to force him to be involved, if he didn't want to be. She didn't want anyone to feel guilted into being part of her life.

When Dad got up and put the kettle on, she realised she was imagining keeping this baby.

The thought – and the anxiety, and the hormones – made her feel sick. And yet... She'd always wanted a family of her own. To be a mother.

But this wasn't how she'd imagined it.

She went to bed early, not able to make conversation, and tossed and turned for hours, imagining possible scenarios. How she might cope. Where she would live. Whether she would be able to afford a baby.

Alfie was rich. She knew that. Maybe she would have to tell him and hope that, even if he didn't want to ever be involved, he would financially support his child.

The full moon shone through a crack in the curtains, and Ivy turned to check the time on her childhood bright pink alarm clock. Three in the morning. Not that long before Dad would be up to help Andy with the cows, really.

Maybe she was writing Alfie off too quickly. She didn't know him that well, really, but everything she did know said that he was a good guy.

So why was she assuming he wouldn't want anything to do with a potential child that he had created?

Because it was a summer fling, she told herself, as she eventually drifted into sleep. *Because there weren't meant to be any strings. And these are the tightest strings*

REBECCA PAULINYI

imaginable.

CHAPTER TWENTY-THREE

When Ivy woke up the next morning after very little sleep, she was struck with a sudden clarity.

She wanted this baby.

She didn't know how it was going to work. She didn't know if she was going to tell Alfie. She didn't know whether she would look back and think it was a crazy decision.

But she wanted this baby.

So she would need to make a doctor's appointment and figure out what the hell she was meant to be doing and get her life together.

The five-year plan was going to have to change – but at least it was for a very good reason.

For three days, she went about her business as usual, throwing up on occasion and trying not to let on that anything had changed. She struggled to talk to Dad in the mornings because the smell of the bacon made her stomach churn, but she managed her deliveries and opened up the shop, and every day Dad was doing more and more work on the farm.

It was all going to be okay.

It had to be.

And then, on Saturday morning, Dad did

something she couldn't ever remember him doing before: he confronted her.

"Ivy," he said, his voice unusually stern, as she scrambled eggs and tried not to breathe in the smell. "Come and sit down."

"What's up, Dad?" she asked with a sigh. "I need to get out to do my deliveries, and–"

"Sit."

His odd behaviour made her a little nervous, and she took the eggs off the heat and sat down at the table. He sat down opposite, and surveyed her for a moment.

"I'm worried about you."

"I'm fine, Dad," Ivy said, trotting out her usual defence.

"You're not. You're pale, and quiet, and racing around...what's the matter?"

She swallowed. Dad noticed more than she had given him credit for. But she wasn't ready to tell him this yet. She needed to have a plan, before she told him she was single and pregnant.

"Nothing. Just been a busy summer, your accident, you know..."

He shook his head. "No. This is from before my accident. Ivy, love, I just want to make sure things are moving in the right direction. I know how hard it was for you, after Jackson left..."

Ivy wished she'd got round to making a cup of tea before she had sat down. Not because she particularly wanted any, but so that she could have something to do instead of answer him.

She'd barely thought about Jackson lately. This had nothing to do with him. Her misery, her stress, how distracted she had been...it had nothing to do with the ex now living miles away with his new girlfriend.

But if she told Dad that, she'd have to explain.

And she didn't want to explain.

"Dad, let's just leave it, please. I'm fine, I promise…"

"You need to move on from him, sweetheart. I know you were with him a long time, and you expected it to last forever, but I don't want you wasting your life pining for a man who I never thought was good enough for you anyway."

Ivy took a deep breath. In some ways, it was nice to hear that Dad thought she was too good for Jackson – but she didn't want to talk about Jackson. Or any of this right now.

"Okay, Dad. I'm moving on, I promise." She got up and put the eggs back on the heat, although they looked rubbery and ruined already. They made her feel even queasier, and she hoped the conversation was over, because she didn't want to have to run out to be sick.

"You're young, Ivy. Don't waste your life pining over him."

Something inside her snapped. She whirled around, seeing red. "I'm not wasting my life, Dad," she spat.

"I didn't mean–"

"What have you done since Mum died? It's been seventeen years, and you've never dated, never remarried, never moved on. You tell me I'm wasting my life pining, but what about you?"

Dad gasped and sat back in his chair, looking momentarily stunned. "Ivy," he said, hurt in his voice. Ivy knew she had gone too far, that she ought to apologise, that none of this was Dad's fault, but fury raged inside her in a way she'd never known before.

"I'm trapped in this place with no plans and no prospects and no one to turn to," she said, tears welling up her eyes. "And all you can do is criticise me."

"I don't think–" Dad began, looking a bit pale himself.

But Ivy couldn't stand in that kitchen any more, with the walls feeling like they were going to close in around her. She dashed out of the front door, tears clouding her vision, only just remembering to grab her car keys as she did so.

She stopped before she got to her car to throw up behind a bush, and then climbed in the driver's seat, sobbing.

What have I done?

Dad's hurt, shocked face filled her mind, but she couldn't go back. She didn't want to break down and tell him everything. And she didn't want to apologise.

And so she drove. She drove to the only place that brought her peace, even if it also reminded her of her heartache.

She sat on Blackpool Sands this time feeling like her heart wasn't just broken – it was shattered.

Jackson was long gone. It was hard to even muster the energy to be miserable about that any more.

Alfie was gone. That one hurt, even though she had known it was coming.

Dad probably hated her. She had flown off the handle, and she knew it. She'd never had so much trouble controlling her emotions before.

And she was going to have a baby.

She leant her head on her knees and listened to the water splashing onto the shore. How had her life changed so dramatically in such a short space of time?

And was the future set to be even more of a disaster?

CHAPTER TWENTY-FOUR

The next week was one of the longest, hardest and most lonely of Ivy's life.

Dad stayed out of her way. She couldn't blame him. She'd been awful to him. But she couldn't bring herself to apologise and make everything all right.

She barely slept, barely ate, and worked as many hours as she could to keep herself busy.

The fact that she was going to keep this baby had become a certain thing in her mind. But there were still so many things she needed to sort out. She wasn't too sure how far along she was – but she hadn't yet got round to ringing the doctors, and finding out what the hell you did when you found out you were pregnant.

Could she stay living at home with Dad? Would he want her to, after their row? And how would he feel about her being a single mother?

He'd never seemed particularly traditional or old-fashioned in his views...but Ivy knew there was a difference between being fine with her staying over at her boyfriend's, and having a baby living in his house for next God knew how many years.

Her dreams of a new business would have to be put on hold. She wondered if she could keep working until the baby came, and then maybe even still do her deliveries, with the baby in tow.

There was so much to think about.

She managed to get Andy to do the delivery to Shore Cove Campsite, because she knew if she saw Christi, she would be invited in for a cup of tea, and Christi would know something was wrong.

And since Christi knew about Alfie too, Ivy thought she might figure something out, or at least drag it out of her.

She couldn't talk about it yet.

Not until there was a plan.

◆ ◆ ◆

Now that she'd decided the beach wasn't to blame for her break-up, she made a beeline for the nearest one every time she was out and wanted to avoid going home to the awkward atmosphere at home.

As they got closer to the end of September, the beaches grew quieter, and the weather more miserable, but Ivy didn't care. She'd missed the best of the beach weather, not wanting to drag up memories of Jackson. Her relationship with her dad was strained, and she was throwing up most days. If the beach gave her a little pleasure, even in the rain and mist and fog, then she was going to take it.

After delivering her last crate in Salcombe, (although studiously avoiding the campsite, which she had added to Andy's rounds, to avoid having to admit anything to Christi) she decided to head down to the beach, to blow away the cobwebs before she headed home.

There was a chill in the air, but she still took off

her shoes and scrunched her toes in the sand. Her mind wandered back to when she had met Christi down on this beach, and had over-shared about her life.

It had been packed that day, full of families enjoying the beautiful sunshine. She'd not known then that she would end up with a firm friendship with Christi.

Just like she hadn't known, that day at the campsite, that something would grow between her and Alfie.

Or that their fling would lead to a baby.

She walked along the length of the beach, and then turned back. There was a sea mist in the air, but she didn't think it was going to rain. Dad would probably be wondering where she was. Or maybe he was glad she was out. The atmosphere at home was pretty terrible, after all.

Ivy stood and looked out to sea, one hand lightly resting on her stomach. She felt so alone. No one knew about this baby. Very few people even knew about Alfie.

And yet she wasn't alone.

She was growing a new life.

She was going to a mother, when she'd had no mother of her own for so very long.

Feeling overwhelmed by life, she sat on the empty beach and let the tears roll down her face.

She was filled with too many conflicting emotions. Fear, misery, excitement, hope. And no one to share them with.

"Ivy?" The sound of her name reverberating through the still air in a deep, masculine voice made her jump. She froze for a moment, then wiped the tears from her eyes, and turned around.

"Oscar," she said, letting out the breath she had

been holding. "You scared me."

"Sorry," he said, flashing her a smile. "Didn't mean to. Are you okay?"

She almost trotted out her usual line – *I'm fine* – but it was hard to do so when he'd just caught her sobbing alone on a misty beach.

So she shrugged. "I will be." How she hoped that was true.

"Christi's been worried about you," he said, walking down the slight incline of the shingle and sitting beside her on the sand. "Since you haven't been doing the deliveries to the campsite, and she hasn't heard back from you…"

Ivy bit her lip. "I've been busy. Sorry. I'll message her back…"

"I'm not here demanding an apology," he said, his dark eyes full of kindness. "And nor would Christi be, for that matter. I just know she's been worried – and I thought it was your car back there, so I thought I'd come and see if everything was okay."

Tears welled in Ivy's eyes just at the thought that he'd cared enough to come and check on her. She hoped he would just think it was irritation from the cool, salty air that was making her eyes glassy.

"I'm sure you're really busy," Ivy said, hoping she could hold it together until he left.

"No one is expecting me," he said. "If you wanted to talk…"

She bit her lip again, harder this time, only stopping when she could taste blood. She was so desperate to talk to someone, to confide in someone, to get some sort of advice outside of the warring voices in her own head…

But was Oscar Reynolds really the right person to open up to? She barely knew him, really. He was Christi's boyfriend. Someone local, who she'd always seen around school.

But not someone who ought to be burdened with everything that was weighing her down.

"If you need more help on the farm, you know we're happy to do whatever we can..."

Ivy shook her head. "You've all been so generous with your time. And Dad's doing loads better, he's out on the farm most days now, and his cast has come off..."

"That's great," Oscar said.

"We had a fight..." The words slipped out before she'd made a conscious decision to tell him.

"I'm no stranger to arguments with dads," Oscar said with a wry smile. "I think me and my dad fought every day until I moved out."

"Dad and I never argue," Ivy said, struggling to hold back her tears. "But he just kept asking what was wrong, and telling me I couldn't keep pining for Jackson, when that's not what it is, but..."

And then it all came flooding out. She had no idea how much Christi had told him, but if he didn't already, by the time he left that beach, he knew more about Ivy's life than anyone else. She told him about Jackson, and how she'd expected a proposal, and how he'd left. She told him about the fling with Alfie, which of course he must have known about, but how much it hurt her heart when he left.

"Wow," Oscar said, drawing lines in the sand with one finger. "You've had a hell of a summer. Especially with your dad's accident, too. No wonder you feel like everything's falling apart."

Ivy nodded. Her eyes wandered out to sea, where a lone fishing boat bobbed on the water in the distance.

Could she tell him?

She needed to get it off her chest.

Even though he couldn't possibly help her.

"And then..." she began, looking back at him, her heart racing. "I found out that I'm pregnant."

"Wow," he said again. He blinked, as though trying to think what to say to that.

And Ivy couldn't blame him. She felt the same.

"It's Alfie's?" he asked.

Ivy nodded.

"Does he know?"

"No one does," Ivy whispered. "Only you. I'm sorry..."

"Hey, what are you sorry for? For what it's worth, I think you should tell him. He seemed like a decent guy to me. And I think he'd want to know, even if it was just a fling..."

They were all thoughts Ivy'd had herself, but it was nice to hear them from someone else. Someone calm and removed from the situation.

"I don't want him to feel like he has to be involved..."

"You didn't make this baby on your own," Oscar said with a shrug. "I'm not saying he needs to be getting down on one knee or be a full-time father or anything. But he's not the man I thought he was if he wants nothing to do with his own child."

A fresh wave of tears threatened to overwhelm Ivy, and she glanced back out to sea to hide them. It wasn't that she wanted Alfie to propose. She wouldn't want to marry someone she barely knew. Having a baby with a man she barely knew probably wasn't the most sensible idea, either – but she couldn't change that now.

She'd always thought she'd be married when she had a baby. Married to Jackson.

And although he wasn't part of the picture in her head any more, she still struggled to imagine doing this alone.

But wasn't that the decision she'd made?

"Thanks, Oscar," she said, giving him a watery smile. "I can't tell you how much I needed to talk to someone."

"Glad to have helped," he said. "Are you okay to drive home? It's starting to get chilly out here, and that mist is only getting thicker..."

She nodded. "Yeah. I'll be fine." She was starting to believe that could be true. "I'll think about what you said...but would you mind not mentioning any of this to Christi? Just for now? I need to get my head straight before I talk to her about it."

He mimed a zipping motion across his lips. "My lips are sealed. And if you want me to talk to Alfie, tell him how a decent man should behave..."

She laughed nervously. She couldn't think of anything more embarrassing, except maybe her dad pushing him into a shotgun wedding.

As a farmer, he did own a shotgun, but she couldn't imagine him forcing poor Alfie down the aisle against his will.

"No, thanks," she said. "I'll figure out what I'm going to do." She still wasn't sure that telling him was the best plan. Well, not until she knew how far along she was and had something concrete to go to him with, at least.

"Well, if you need to talk – you know where I am. Or

we are. Or whatever, really," Oscar said, running a hand through his hair.

"Thank you, Oscar." She gave him a hug, even though it wasn't something they normally did, because she was so grateful to him for listening. "I really mean it."

She felt lighter as she drove home than she had done since finding out about the baby.

She just needed to make a plan.

Make up with Dad was number one. Then make a doctor's appointment. And then decide on what, if anything, to tell Alfie.

Was it fair to keep him entirely in the dark about his own child?

And what would she do if he did come back down to Devon, and saw her with a kid the perfect age to be his?

Plagued with such complicated questions, the drive back home seemed to take no time at all.

She took a deep breath before opening the front door. Part of her hoped Dad was still out on the farm, so she would have longer to compose herself. But she knew it would be better to get it over with before she lost her nerve and they had another evening of awkward silence.

He wasn't in the kitchen, but when she went through to the living room, she found him sitting in his armchair, his eyes closed. She didn't want to disturb his rest, and so she turned to go back to the kitchen.

"Ivy?"

"Sorry," she said, turning back to find his eyes wide open now. "I didn't mean to wake you."

"It's fine. Wasn't properly asleep. Just being lazy."

Ivy took a seat on the sofa opposite him. "You need to recover still, Dad. It's not lazy."

"Have you been delivering?" he asked.

She nodded. "And took a walk on the beach."

"That's nice." An awkward silence bubbled up and Ivy forced herself to break it.

"I'm really sorry, Dad," she began.

"It's fine, I wasn't really asleep," he said, sitting up straighter.

Ivy shook her head. "No. Not about that. About... everything. What I said to you." Tears began to roll down her cheeks. "I was horrible. And I didn't mean it. I'm sorry, Dad, please forgive me..."

Her dad stood up, and took a seat beside her, pulling her into a one-armed hug. "Of course I do. And I'm sorry, too. I didn't mean to suggest you were wasting your life. I'm just worried..."

Ivy nodded, wiping away her tears with her sleeve. "I know. It's been a really rough summer. But I promise I'm over Jackson. And I'm going to be okay. I have a plan." She couldn't face telling him about the baby just yet, but she knew she would have to fairly soon.

"I never wanted you to feel trapped here..."

"I don't." Ivy took his hand and squeezed it. "I chose to stay here. I was in a bad mood, and I said things I didn't mean. Please, forget it all."

Dad swallowed. "The stuff about your mum..."

"Dad..." Ivy groaned, burying her face in her hands.

"I never thought you would want me to get remarried," he said. "And if I'm honest, I don't know if I could ever love someone like I loved your mother."

"I know Dad. I shouldn't have said that. I was angry and feeling frustrated at...everything. And I took it out on you. I'm sorry."

Dad pulled her into a tight hug, and she buried her head in his shoulder. "I love you, Ivy. I just want you to be happy."

"I know," Ivy said through a sob. "And I will be. I promise."

CHAPTER TWENTY-FIVE

After going through her dates with the midwife for the third time, they were both pretty sure she was ten weeks pregnant – although they couldn't know for definite until the scan, which was booked in for the following week.

Even discussing it with a healthcare professional didn't make it seem totally real. She let the midwife take her blood and ask medical history questions, and even managed not to cry when she had to tell her that she knew nothing of the medical history of the father.

Was the midwife judging her? She didn't seem to be, outwardly, but Ivy was just pleased she wasn't someone she recognised from the shop or from living in the area so long.

A little anonymity wasn't a bad thing.

The following Wednesday, still undecided about whether she was going to tell Alfie, she decided to deliver to the campsite herself. She wanted to see Christi. She wasn't sure if she was going to tell her everything, but avoiding her friend wasn't doing anyone any good.

She expected to be dragged in for a cup of tea, presuming her friend was at the campsite – but she did not expect to come up the drive and find herself stopped by Alfie's black sports car.

She swore in her head and her blood ran cold in her veins.

Why was he here?

Had Oscar told him?

Was she going to have to tell him everything, right now, without having prepared?

She did consider quickly reversing down the drive and pretending she'd never come, but Christi came running out before she had a chance. Slowly, Ivy got out of the car, and tried to make her thoughts stop racing for long enough to decide what she was going to say.

"Alfie's here," Christi said, a little breathlessly, once she was close enough to speak.

"Why?"

"Something to do with his parents' house."

Ivy's pulse slowed a little. If he knew about the baby, he hadn't told Christi about it at least.

"I know how upset you were at him leaving," Christi said. "If you want to go, before he sees you…"

Part of Ivy wanted to run, to not have to face him right now. But a bigger part of her was drawn to him. In the three weeks since he had gone, she had missed him more than she could have imagined.

Seeing him briefly would undoubtedly be painful.

But would it be better than not seeing him at all?

He appeared in the cottage doorway before she had time to make a decision, and her heart skipped a beat.

He looked the same. After all, not much time had passed. But she felt like a different person.

"You okay?" Christi asked.

Ivy nodded. Her mouth had gone dry and she was very afraid she was going to make a total fool of herself. He raised his hand to wave and she waved back, her hand feeling as heavy as lead.

"Want to come in for a cup of tea?" Christi asked.

"Yeah. Go on then."

She walked towards the cottage, her heart racing. He couldn't know. He wouldn't be standing there so calmly if he did, surely. And if Christi knew, she was sure she would have found a way to ask her.

Oscar must have kept her secret.

She just had to decide when she was going to be ready to share it with the rest of the world.

Christi slid past Alfie into the cottage, saying something about putting the kettle on, and leaving Ivy and the breathtakingly handsome blond alone together outside.

"Hey," he said, and that one word made her heart feel like it was about to jump from her chest.

She was definitely in way deeper than she had planned to be.

"Hi." She twirled a loose piece of hair around her finger like a teenager in secondary school, talking to her crush with no idea what to say. "Fancied some more camping?"

He laughed. "I'm staying at my parents' place, actually."

"Oh, right," Ivy said. "Of course. In Hope Cove. Is everything okay? Christi said there was something you had to sort…"

Alfie ran a hand through his thick hair, but it only seemed to fall more into his eyes as he did so. "Yeah, just something with the pipes, and…" He bit his bottom lip, and Ivy had to ignore the urge to stand on tiptoes and kiss him.

They weren't in a relationship.

They were nothing.

Even if she was carrying his baby.

"Ivy, I haven't been able to stop thinking about you."

Ivy blinked in shock. "What?"

"I know it was just a summer fling, and I don't know what the hell I'm thinking or how this would ever work, but there's nothing wrong with the house. It was an excuse, to come down and see you."

"Oh." She couldn't think of anything else to say. He'd been on her mind since he left, but she'd never dreamed that the reverse was true.

He'd come all the way back to see her again?

Butterflies filled her stomach at the thought, but the black clouds of reality drew closer. Would he feel the same, once he knew she was pregnant? And even if he did, he had already admitted he didn't know what the outcome of this could possibly be. He was here, but for how long?

"I should have rung," Alfie said, shifting his weight between his feet. "I know how pathetic this sounds. I just wanted to see you. But I know it was just a summer thing, and just turning up like this, disrupting your life…"

Ivy almost laughed. He certainly had disrupted her life – but not in the way he thought.

"I wanted to see you too," she said, because it was the truth. "I don't know how sensible that is…"

He bent down and pressed a brief kiss to her lips, and heat flooded through her body.

"I don't care about being sensible right now," he said.

"Kettle's boiled!" Christi's voice floated out of the open door.

"Mind if I stay for a cup of tea, too? I don't want to make things awkward..."

"Of course not," Ivy said, enjoying the moment of joy while it lasted. "But then maybe we could go for a walk, and talk?"

Just as autumn always rolled around to bring summer to a close, this moment of joy would have to end with the most difficult conversation of Ivy's life.

CHAPTER TWENTY-SIX

They walked to the top of the campsite, where the hot tub looking out to sea was still in operation, but not in use. The field still had a smattering of tents across it, but once the October half-term came and went, the campsite would be closed until Easter.

Alfie took her hand as they sat down on the bench and watched the clouds blowing over the sea.

"How have you been?" he asked. "I wanted to text and ask, but I didn't know if I could..."

"You could have done," Ivy said, enjoying the warmth of his hand around hers.

"I know I'm probably coming on a bit strong. And if you want me not to come back again, you only have to say..."

She squeezed his hand. "I'm really happy to see you."

"I thought I could take you on a proper date. And then we can figure all of this out. I don't want to just have a fling with you, with no strings – I want to see if this could go anywhere. I know the distance is an issue..."

A sob caught in Ivy's throat. The distance wasn't the only issue.

This handsome, funny, sexy man wanted to date

her, and yet he lived hours away, and he was totally unaware that she was pregnant.

There could be no casual dating for them. No having fun and seeing where things led.

They could only go straight to serious, because there was going to be a baby involved.

"Alfie..." she said, her voice breaking a little. She had to tell him, and she had to tell him now. She hadn't even decided that morning whether or not he needed to know – but now it was clear that he did.

She had a vision of how everything could have been. Of Alfie coming back, and them going out on dates, and away for the weekend, and figuring out something long-distance between them. Seeing where things went without any pressure. None of that was an option any more.

"I didn't mean to upset you," he said, looking confused.

"I know. It's just..." She squeezed her eyes shut for a moment, and forced the words out. "Alfie, I found out... not very long ago..." She bit her bottom lip, unable to look at him as she said the words that had the power to change his life forever: "I'm pregnant."

He didn't let go of her hand, but he didn't say anything, either. When the silence became awkward, she looked up at him, and saw his features frozen in surprise.

"It's your baby," she added, realising she hadn't made that clear. "I'm sorry, I know this is all a shock, I... I didn't know how to tell you."

The tears that had threatened to fall seemed to have abated. In fact, she felt oddly calm and detached from the situation, as she watched the emotions play across Alfie's handsome face. Surprise. Shock. Fear.

All the feelings she'd had herself.

Alfie cleared his throat. "What—" His voice was a little hoarse, and he cleared it and tried again. "Have you decided what you want to do?" he asked. "I thought we were pretty careful…"

Ivy shrugged. "Not careful enough, it seems. I think… I think I want to keep it," she said, her voice dropping to a soft whisper. "I've seen a midwife. Worked out my dates. I haven't told Dad yet, not sure how he's going to react."

She realised she was wittering on, but she'd never known Alfie so quiet. She felt the need to fill the silence.

"I don't expect anything from you," she said when he still had nothing to say. She wondered if she should remove her hand from his, but he was still holding on, and there was some comfort to be had from that contact.

She felt as though Alfie might bolt at any moment.

Of course he was shocked. But she'd expected a bit more from him than a blank, terrified expression.

"That's not—" Alfie began. "I mean… I just…"

Ivy wanted to cry. She didn't know what she'd expected from Alfie, when she'd dropped this bombshell, but somehow, him knowing about the baby and being unable to say anything supportive made her feel even more alone than before.

Oscar had known what to say to her, when she'd cried to him on the beach. But then it wasn't his baby. It wasn't going to impact his life at all.

"I think I'm going to go," Ivy said softly, pulling her hand from Alfie's. He didn't resist. "Bye, Alfie."

She was halfway down the hill by the time she heard him call her name. But the tears had started to flow, and she didn't want to turn back and have him see.

He knew now. He could process, and decide whether he wanted to know his baby. Ivy had to focus on herself now. Herself, and the life she was growing.

She didn't really know Alfie, she told herself as she drove home in tears. That was the problem. When the going was good, of course he'd been the perfect gentleman.

How would Jackson have reacted, if she'd told him she was pregnant? The question stuck in her mind all the way home. He probably would have bombarded her with questions that made her feel like she'd done something wrong.

Another decision was made for her as she pulled up to the farmhouse. There was no way she could sneak inside without Dad seeing her, and fix her make-up so that she could hide that she'd been crying – because he was outside already, sitting on the wooden bench outside the front door and pulling off his Wellington boots.

CHAPTER TWENTY-SEVEN

"Ivy?" Dad said, standing up with a concerned look on his face and only one boot on. "What's happened?"

Ivy closed the car door and took a deep breath. She didn't want to lie to him any more. She didn't want to hide this. She had made her choice – and she didn't want to be alone.

"Can we have a cup of tea?" she asked. "And talk?"

"You know we can always talk, love."

"I'll put the kettle on – don't come in with that boot on," Ivy said with a half-laugh.

As the kettle boiled, she tried to decide how she was going to tell him. She had no idea how he was going to react. They'd never fallen out, aside from the one, terrible, big row which had shaken Ivy to her core.

"You're scaring me a little, sweetheart," Dad said, taking a seat at the kitchen table as Ivy poured the boiling water into two mugs.

"I…" She sat down, trying to figure out where to start. "Over the summer, I was seeing someone," she said. He needed a little context, before she just announced she was pregnant.

"Okay," Dad said, looking confused. "And he's hurt you?"

Ivy shook her head. "No. Well. Not really. He's a friend of Christi's. He was only here for the summer. It was a short-term thing. After Jackson..."

Dad nodded, and waited for her to continue.

"When he left, I found it harder than I thought." It wasn't really relevant, but she hoped Dad might put two and two together and realise why she had been in such a terrible mood. "And then..."

This was it. The moment of truth. Once out, the words could never be taken back. "I realised I'm pregnant."

Dad's mouth formed an O, and he tightened his grip around his tea.

"This obviously wasn't planned, and I have been agonising over it, but I think... I think I want to keep the baby. I don't know how I'm going to manage it yet, but that's what I want to do."

Every time the words came out of her mouth, she found she was more sure.

"Does the father know?"

Ivy nodded. "I've told him, and that I don't expect anything from him..."

"He shouldn't just walk away from this."

Ivy didn't want to talk about Alfie. If she did, she was sure she'd just start crying again. "He may not. I'm going to give him time and space to figure out what he wants to do. But I've made this decision for myself, and if I have to do it alone, I will," she said.

"You won't be alone, Ivy," Dad said, letting go of his mug of tea and taking her hand. "I'll support you, no matter what. I'll help you raise a baby, even though it's been a very long time since I've even held one. You can stay living here for as long as you want – whatever you need. I'm here for you." He squeezed her hand, tightly. "Always."

"Oh Dad," she said, tears pricking her eyes. "Thank you." She reached for him, hugging him tightly. He didn't always know what to say, but in this moment, he'd said exactly what she'd needed to hear. That he was there for her. That he would help her. That she didn't have to be alone.

She had no idea how this was all going to work out. Her five-year plan would certainly have to alter drastically.

But she had a path to follow. It wasn't the one she had imagined, but that didn't mean it wasn't the right path for her.

She'd felt so lonely, and yet she'd had the support she was looking for all along, right at home with her.

Dad had been her only family for so long, and now she was expanding that family. No, it wasn't the way she had pictured it. But that didn't mean it couldn't work.

◆ ◆ ◆

After staying up late talking everything through with Dad, Ivy felt more at peace the following morning than she had done in a long time. She hadn't heard from Alfie, but she wasn't going to dwell on that.

She had bigger things to focus on.

She'd thought her life was heading in one very specific direction, and Jackson had pulled the rug from underneath her and sent her careering off on another path. And now she was on another path entirely, and she was determined to learn how to walk it alone.

With Dad happy to support her, and the fact that she would be able to continue deliveries and running the shop, she wasn't so anxious about the future. Dad was back at work, and her plans for a café would just have to be postponed.

She was young. There was time to do it all.

Once she'd eaten breakfast with Dad – well, pushed some food around her plate and tried not to throw up – she decided to go for a walk, to get her head straight. The shop was closed, and Andy was doing the day's deliveries.

She drove to Blackpool Sands without really thinking about it. Was Alfie still at the campsite? She couldn't help but wonder. Did Christi know about the baby yet? She would sit down with her friend soon, and talk it through.

But for today, she just wanted to clear her mind. To let all the stress fall away, and focus on the positives.

She was going to be a mother.

It was something she had always wanted, and however it had come about, it was now in motion.

And she had a father who would do anything for her. That was something to celebrate.

There was a light sea breeze on the beach, and white clouds filled the sky, but it didn't seem like it was going to rain. Ivy slipped her shoes off and dug her toes into the sand as soon as she was able, letting out a sigh of relief.

She wandered along the beach, thinking of her own mother. She didn't like to dwell on how much she missed her. Ivy always tried to be a positive person, and thinking about how much she missed her mum didn't help with that.

But right now, she wished she could speak to her even more than she normally did. That she could tell her about this baby. That she could ask for her advice.

But that wasn't possible. So she would have to be content with walking along her favourite beach in the world; the place where she felt the closest to her mum. The place where she remembered swimming and picnicking and digging giant holes.

Although there was nothing visible there yet, her hand rested on her stomach, and she looked out to sea, breathing in the salty air.

This was where she belonged.

The breeze caught her long hair, which she hadn't bothered to plait, and she closed her eyes, enjoying the feeling of all the cobwebs being blown away.

"Ivy?"

At first she thought she'd imagined it. A voice on the wind that her mind had conjured up.

And then it came again, stronger. "Ivy."

She turned to see Alfie walking down the beach towards her, his blond hair blowing around his face, his hands in his jeans pockets.

Ivy wanted to feel calm, to tell herself it meant nothing, to not open herself up to any more heartbreak.

But her heart flipped in her chest anyway.

He waited until he was beside her, the waves lapping at the shore behind them, to speak again. "Your dad said I might find you here."

"You met my dad?" Ivy said, immediately panicking about what Dad might have said.

"Yeah. He didn't look very impressed to see me…"

Ivy bit her lip.

"I told him, about the baby. So he probably assumes…"

"I don't blame him," Alfie said. "Ivy… I'm really sorry about yesterday."

Ivy looked up into his sparkling blue eyes and wished her hair was tied back so that she didn't have to keep pushing it from her face.

"I was in shock," he said.

"I understand."

"I shouldn't have just frozen, though. That was wrong of me. You're in shock about this, too. Neither of us planned it."

"I'd had a bit more time to get my head around it, though," Ivy said. She'd not wanted to make excuses for him before, but now, falling from his own beautiful lips, they sounded reasonable.

"I should have reacted better. I'm not just going to disappear into thin air, I promise you."

He smiled at her, and she couldn't help but smile back. There was something about his boyish grin that made her heart race, no matter the situation.

"I want to be part of this child's life, Ivy. And yours, too, if you'll have me."

The wind whipped Ivy's hair backwards as she gasped at his words. Her mouth felt dry and her heart raced. She hadn't expected to see him today. And she hadn't expected him to want *her* still.

"I'm not saying let's get married or anything, because I think marrying someone you barely know is a recipe for disaster," he said, running a hand through his thick hair. "But I would like us to give this a go."

"What are you thinking, exactly?" Ivy said, wetting her lips with her tongue and tasting salt.

"I haven't had time to think it all through," he said. "But I could move down here, part-time at least. Work remotely, while we figure things out. We could try dating properly, if you wanted…"

Ivy nodded without even thinking about it.

"And then when the baby comes, we'll raise it together."

"You're sure?" Ivy asked. "Moving down here, even part-time…that's huge."

Alfie gave a half-smile. "Not as huge as having a baby. But I think we should give it a go. I don't know if it will work, or how it will work, but I want you to know that you're not going to have to do this alone. No matter what."

Ivy's heart was so full of joy that she thought it might burst. He took her hands, and pulled her closer, and as the waves inched closer, washing over Ivy's feet and Alfie's black trainers, he bent his head and pressed his lips to hers.

Ivy struggled to picture what her future would look like, or how parenthood and dating the father of her child would pan out. But in that moment, on Blackpool Sands beach, she felt as though her broken heart was on its way to being whole again.

◆ ◆ ◆

Is a fake relationship the best way to silence Hannah's nagging parents when they attend a family wedding in the beautiful village of Hope Cove?

Return to Devon and witness the wedding of the summer season, and a chance meeting that might just change Hannah and Anthony's lives for good… mybook.to/HopeCove

AFTERWORD

Thank you so much for reading 'Broken-Hearted on Blackpool Sands'. It features some more of my favourite places South Devon, and while the businesses are all fictitious, the locations are very much real.

While the South West of England doesn't always enjoy glorious weather, we are right now as I write this, and I would love to be able to take a dip in the sea - even though I know it would be freezing!

You can catch up with all these characters and more in the next book of the 'Dreaming of Devon' series: 'Happily Ever After in Hope Cove' (mybook.to/HopeCove). This features the wedding of one of our favourite couples, and a new romance too!

Thank you so much for your support. Reviews are really appreciated and make a real difference! You can also sign up for my newsletter at tiny.cc/paulinyi to hear about sales, news, and my photos of beautiful Devon!
Thanks again for being here, your support means so much to me!

Happy reading,

Rebecca

DREAMING OF DEVON

Travel to the beautiful South West coast of England and fall in love with the landscapes, the people, and their journeys in life.

Sunsets Over Salcombe

A tiny flat. A dead-end job. High-flying siblings.

Christi King is used to being the disappointment of the family. Not that anyone would say it out loud. But when redundancy encourages her to spend the summer at her aunt's Devon campsite, she's forced to face the fact that her life is not going the way she had planned.

And nor is Aunt Olivia's campsite. Even with the help of local handyman Oscar, it's not earning enough to pay the bills.

If Christi can turn things around, perhaps she can prove that she is more capable than anyone thinks. She throws herself into small town life, feeling free in the space after years of feeling cramped and stressed.

When she is offered a new start, will Devon, Aunt Olivia, and Oscar give her a reason to stay?

Broken-Hearted On Blackpool Sands

Ivy Thompson has always been a romantic.

And when her boyfriend plans a romantic walk and a picnic on the most beautiful beach in Devon, Ivy is sure she'll end the day with a proposal.

Never in her wildest dreams did she expect to watch the sun set with a broken heart and no ring upon her finger.

Ivy throws herself into her work, into the village she has grown up in, into the excitement of a summer fling with a visitor at the local campsite.

She doesn't know what her life holds any more – but keeping busy takes away some on the pain.

Romance is the last thing on her mind.

Her summer of fun must come to an end… Will Ivy still be broken-hearted on Blackpool Sands when autumn rolls around?

Happily Ever After In Hope Cove

A family wedding is the last way Hannah wants to spend a rare weekend off. Especially with her parents constantly asking when she's going to settle down and give them grandkids.

Why can't they understand that her career as a doctor is

all she can think about right now?

At her cousin Oscar's wedding, she's desperate to shut them up – and so grabs the nearest handsome man and kisses him, hoping he'll be willing to pretend to be her date for the day.

What she doesn't know is that he's the bride's brother – and that he's just as fed up of his parents match-making as she is.

Pretending to be together becomes an easy way to silence their parents whenever they travel down to family events in Devon – until an ex comes back into the picture, and jealousy surprisingly rears its ugly head.

Will both families figure out the ruse – or can a fake relationship, across hundreds of miles, turn into something more?

BOOKS BY THIS AUTHOR

The Worst Christmas Ever?

Can the magic of the Christmas season be rediscovered in a small Devon town?

When Shirley 'Lee' Jones returns home from an awful day at the office, the last thing she expects to find is her husband in bed with another woman. Six weeks until Christmas, and Lee finds the life she had so carefully planned has been utterly decimated.

Hurt, angry and confused, Lee makes a whirlwind decision to drive her problems away and ends up in Totnes, an eccentric town in the heart of Devon. As Christmas approaches, Lee tries to figure out what path her life will follow now, as she looks at it from the perspective of a soon-to-be 31-year-old divorcée.

Can she ever return to her normal life? Or is a new reality - and a new man - on the horizon?

Finding herself and flirting with the handsome local police officer might just make this the best Christmas ever.

Fans of Jill Mansell and Sophie Kinsella are loving this romantic series.

Buy 'The Worst Christmas Ever?' and begin your journey to Devon today!

Lawyers And Lattes

Feeling The Fireworks

The Best Christmas Ever

Trouble In Tartan

Summer Of Sunshine

Healing The Heartbreak

Dancing Till Dawn

At The Stroke Of Thirty

Life Begins At Thirty

Printed in Great Britain
by Amazon